Mosi-oa-Tunya

THE THUNDERING SMOKE

BOOK TWO
THE DUTCHMAN'S PLAN

GUY QUIGLEY

ISBN 978-1-967421-19-0 (Paperback)
ISBN 978-1-967421-20-6 (Hardback)
ISBN 978-1-967421-18-3 (eBook)

Printed in the United States of America

Published by ThunderSmoke Media LLC

DEDICATION

This book is dedicated to my wonderful wife Wendy, a true child of Africa, my soul mate, partner, mother of my children, and best friend for over fifty-four years.

ACKNOWLEDGEMENTS

To my parents, Joseph Quigley and Mother Josephine Quigley, the ultimate thespians. He was a violin virtuoso who was as comfortable playing the classics as he was an Irish jig. While she was an exceptional actress/director who could watch a film and later write the script from memory. These guiding lights taught me the art of self-expression. Without their love, knowledge, encouragement, and early guidance, this novel may never have been possible (RIP)

AND

To my mother-in-law, Stella Horton, a sophisticated lady and healer with significant hands-on knowledge about Africa and its wildlife. Also, thanks to my father-in-law George Horton, the finest hunter I have ever known with bush skills that were unquestionable. I savor those many nights spent around a roaring campfire while lions mated in the distance, hearing countless true stories stranger than fiction. And to the many collectively unknown who helped shape this story. (RIP)

AND

A very special thank you to my eldest daughter Claudine Quigley Piechotta, who embarked on the amazing and time-consuming challenge of editing and adapting this manuscript. With her input and prowess, she painlessly and graciously undertook the task of rewriting my manuscript. A very special and talented lady.

ABOUT THE AUTHOR

Guy Quigley was born in Ireland to a second-generation thespian family. He was educated in Ireland, where he left the theatre and entered the business world. He is married with three children and has six grandchildren. From 1970 through the early 80s, he built a 40,000-acre cattle ranch in Zambia, Africa housing 5,000 heads of cattle and imported 100 pedigree Semmintaler cattle from Bavaria, Germany, via three Boeing 707 Skybarn aircraft, establishing the first pedigree Semmintaler stud in the south-central African country.

In his spare time, he wrote two fictional novels — one, a children's story, *The Little People*, and the other, a historical fiction saga, *The Smoke That Thunders*; now after over forty years is being published as a trilogy.

In the United States, he successfully developed and marketed an award-winning cold remedy zinc lozenge under the franchise name COLD-EEZE,® establishing the US zinc-lozenge marketplace. To market the product, he formed The Quigley Corporation in 1989 which became a public entity on February 7, 1991, trading on the NASDAQ under the symbol (QGLY). His product COLD-EEZE® is available throughout the United States. He retired in 2009 and returned to his writing which has been of tremendous therapeutic value and comes full circle to his birth roots. He has written three more books, *The Rebel Son with an* (Audio Book), *Hellevator* and a soon to be published cold-war spy thriller *Predators at the Gates,* which will also be available as an audio book. Along with his novels, he has written several award-winning movie scripts. In his film production endeavors, He is the ex-producer of *Magic Boys* (*Diamond Heist*) in the EU. He is also the ex-producer of the spoof *Breaking Wind* and the ex-producer of *Wicked Blood*. Utilizing his ThunderSmoke Media Company he produced the 2015 award-winning movie *Apparition*. His latest film production from ThunderSmoke Media is *Impuratus*, a thriller horror movie, due for release in North America and world-wide distribution in October 2023.

www.guyquigley.com www.thundersmokefilms.com

PREFACE

For over a decade, along with my wife, I owned and operated a cattle ranch in the south-central African country of Zambia. Without TV and little reliable world news, we were somewhat cloistered and spent most evenings listening to true stories dating back to the last century. Coming from an Irish thespian background did not make me the ideal worker of the land, yet I learned the hard way by trial and error.

My motivation to write a book stemmed from the endless stories I learned. Hence, at every spare moment I had, I started to handwrite my story utilizing my knowledge of Ireland, her history, and the Africa I came to know and love and attempted to weave them together in an action-adventure love story. After a couple of chapters, it all seemed to fall into place, and I could not wait to put more words on paper, albeit they were barely legible from my terrible art of scribbling.

So was born my story of a fictional character called Tom Sutton, who, during the Irish liberation war of 1919, under the inspiration of Michael Collins – the top Irish revolutionary leader of the time – was overtly successful in his execution of disrupting British rule. Being a man with a price on his head, he loses his wife Grace - the love of his life - in a brutal rape executed by Black and Tans at a bloody raid on his home.

Believing his son Sean suffered the same deadly fate as Grace, he is forced to escape, and by sheer misunderstanding, he finds himself on the vast continent of Africa, sinking into the shame and degradation of alcohol. By a strange twist of fate, a little girl with a bowl of soup and the fear of the loss of her dying father brings him back from living death to the reality of the child's pain and future.

Together with the young girl Heidi and Weasel Byrne, his only friend from the troubled Irish times, they travel north through the small working goldmines of Southern Rhodesia to the north of Mosi-oa-Tunya (The Smoke That Thunders-Victoria falls), finally settling in Northern Rhodesia. There, a new life of intrigue, crime, adventure, and love is born until his past comes back to haunt him.

My problem in writing a novel was the fact that it was handwritten and two-finger typed. There were no computers back in the mid-seventies, so errors abounded. It took over eighteen months to get my writing into some form of a legible manuscript. So, what did I learn from such an experience? Patience is definitely a virtue.

The story, in my mind, was chapters ahead of what was being handwritten. Several times, there was writer's block. That taught me to think hard and continue to write, even if nobody liked it. This book was my first attempt at writing, and since then, I have written two other books and several screenplays.

CONTENTS

CHAPTER 1

THE DUTCHMAN'S PLAN

The rain pelted the long window of the Grand Station Hotel, two stories above the busy city street. The rainy season had arrived in Johannesburg with gusto, and humidity hung in the air like hot breath. Back in Ireland, families would be preparing for Christmas now, Tom thought with a tinge of melancholy. For a moment, he saw Sean sitting on that threadbare rug on Christmas morning, grinning from ear to ear, enchanted with his new toy lorry and bag of marbles. Sean's toys morphed into the piles of books and maps strewn on the floor before him, and the snowy cottage faded from Tom's mind.

It had been a month since Heidi had returned to the orphanage in Cape Town. A few days after her departure, Tom had been released from the hospital, and Weasel had moved him into his hotel room at the behest of their employer so that Tom could fully recover before returning to the mine. It was a happy place full of natural light and alive with the bustle of travelers in and around it. Two stylish single beds with carved headboards and down pillows stood against the pink rose-patterned wallpaper separated by a nightstand and table lamp. Two Victorian armchairs with velvet cushions and a dark wooden pedestal coffee table rounded out the room. From Tom's armchair, he could see into the adjoining modern bathroom, complete with a commode, porcelain tub, and oval sink engraved in a similar floral pattern repeated in the wallpaper and bedroom curtains.

Tom had required no incentive to stay here. The city was a willing participant in his mission. If he was going to attempt to adopt Heidi, he had to create a believable backstory that might convince the orphanage of his honorable intentions. He quickly became friendly with the librarian at the Johannesburg City Library and spent several hours a day pouring over books on farming and studying the topography of Northern Rhodesia in maps, committing as much to memory as he could. When he wasn't reading, Tom hung around the station house, befriending any Rhodesian who might step onto the platform. He managed to coax a few into a drink at the hotel under the guise that he was a newspaperman writing a story about Rhodesian farmers and then would take copious notes as the travelers waxed on about their adventures over a free whisky or beer. He was determined to become at least a theoretical expert on the region. His charm, he hoped, would take off the rest.

The door clicked open, and Weasel stood in the doorway soaked to the skin, carrying a crate of brown bottles. He offered the standard look of disapproval as Tom released a puff of cigar smoke into the air over his copy of *"The Story of an African Farm" by Olive Schreiner.* Amused, Tom gave Weasel a large grin and took another pull off his cigar with satisfaction. Weasel set down the dark blue crate and peeled off his wet jacket, letting it drop to the floor. He decided to not lecture Tom on his cigar smoking today.

"Want one?" Weasel asked, pulling out the familiar red labeled dark amber bottle, beads of sweat running down its side.

They had been introduced to Castle lager by their Swedish employer, who extolled the virtues of the beer, and of course, its Swedish brewer Anders Ohlsson. It didn't hold a candle to Guinness, the Irishmen had decided, but it wasn't bad, especially on a humid African day.

"Yes, please," said Tom putting out his cigar. "...and Weasel, once you dry off, I'd like to discuss something with you."

Weasel flopped on the chair opposite Tom, rubbing his wet hair furiously with a towel. Then both men leaned in and clinked their bottles absentmindedly. *"Slainte,"* they said in comradery and took a long swig from their beers.

"So, what's going on, Tom?" Weasel said, crossing his legs on the table between them.

"I want to talk about Heidi."

"I figured you did. It's not like I haven't noticed how seriously you've been studying up these past two weeks."

"I cannot abandon her," Tom said seriously, staring out the window with a faraway look.

"I thought maybe if you saw her again and we could work out a way to have visits with the lass, that it would be enough. Ugh, I knew it would come to this. Tom, you know it's a liability to have a child at your age."

"Weasel, had Sean been here, he would've been ten years old. Why do you doubt my parenting skills?"

"I don't doubt your paternal abilities, Tom. But let me put it this way. Do you want to be a father to that particular little girl?"

"Bloody hell, I do. Weasel, I was a father once."

"I'm not saying that. I'm asking if you know what you're getting yourself into with that little fireball."

The thought of Heidi's industriousness and confidence made them both laugh out loud.

"So, I suppose we are going through with the story about us being farmers from Northern Rhodesia? Do you think you have your story straight?

"You know I had this planned all along, didn't you? Tom said with a grin, "…to adopt Heidi…that's why I sent you after all."

"I can see that your mind is made up, but I hope you have thought this through, Thomas. Even if they agree to an adoption by a single man, it is not a matter of a day, week, or month. It is a child's life. You're committing to raise her until the day she gets married. That could be ten, fifteen, or more years from now. Recognize that you're removing the child from a safe place."

"I know."

"Make sure this is not just because you feel empathy for her or that you're trying to make amends for your own loss."

This struck a chord with Tom, and he stamped out his cigar in frustration, rose, and started pacing around the room. He rounded on Weasel angrily.

"You stopped me from going back to my wife and son. And I know you did it to save my life, but you will never understand the guilt I feel for not being there when they needed me the most. Heidi brought me out of that misery, and then you made me leave her, and she was forced to grieve alone. Don't you see that she has shown me that my life can have meaning again, and in turn, I can offer her a chance at a family and a real life outside an institution? I won't deny that, in some way, I feel like this is repentance for Grace and Sean's deaths. But don't deny me the chance to find some redemption in this life, Weasel."

Weasel melted in the chair before him because he knew that his friend was immovable. He was resolute, and if they were to stay friends, brothers, he had only one option: help him adopt Heidi.

"You're going to be the bloody death of me, Sutton." Weasel conceded.

Tom sat back down in his chair, grabbed his abandoned beer, and took a gulp. "I'm heading to Cape Town tomorrow."

Weasel sighed and took a gulp of his beer, raising the bottle in a toast. "So, when are we leaving then?" The men clinked their beer bottles to seal the agreement.

The next morning, they dressed early and made their way to the train station. Tom brought along his maps and a couple of books to review on the train ride. Tom got Weasel up to speed on some of the essential points in their masquerade, drilling him on dates and places to make sure they had it memorized verbatim. Weasel bemoaned the idea of having to stay at Baldwin's boarding house, an establishment he had hoped to never see the inside of again, mostly due to its proprietor. Tom agreed and insisted that they find another lodging. He was convinced that they may have to stay in Cape Town for a while anyway to prove to the orphanage and its administrator that his intent was honorable. He hoped that familiarity would eventually wear Koning down.

As they disembarked the train, Weasel remembered the weird encounter he had had with a small bald man before he left Cape Town with Heidi. He had completely put it out of his mind until he saw the bench where they had waited for the train.

"I completely forgot this to tell you, Sutton. Before you head off to visit Heidi, there's a solicitor that wants to meet you."

"Who are you talking about?"

"Oh, just some odd little man. Honestly, I had put it out of my mind. He accosted Heidi and me here when we were waiting for the train to Joburg. He said something about the Dutchman, and his last wish was to have you meet him or some malarkey. Wilkinson, yes, his name was Wilkinson. He said his office was right across the street from the orphanage."

"That's strange...but let's focus on getting ourselves some lodging today. We'll go there first thing tomorrow before we visit Heidi. Oh, I also want to get Heidi a little present...it is almost Christmas."

Tom and Weasel spent the remainder of the day looking for a flat to let. By evening, they had settled into a shabby one-bedroom flat three stories up and a few streets away from the orphanage. Tom had bought a leather-bound copy of Peter Pan for Heidi, one of Sean's favorites. He was excited to give it to her and laid the brown parcel on the table next to the double bed that he and Weasel had to share for however many weeks this endeavor took. Tom hung his suit carefully in the wardrobe while Weasel took off his trousers and placed them beneath the mattress to iron out the creases before he sprawled out on the well-worn cotton sheet.

"Bloody hell, I wonder what this Wilkinson wants from me?" said Tom reviving the conversation as he spit-polished his shoes for the next day.

"How would I know? I'm taking the right side of the bed, Tom. You can sleep on the left."

"Suit yourself. Don't mind me. I'm just going to recite my speech for tomorrow."

Tom pulled out a cigar and lit it, allowing thick gray clouds to waft above Weasel. In response to the all too familiar scowl, Tom moved to the open window as he continued to recite his monologue extolling the virtues of farm life.

"You know, sometimes I'd much rather have you as a bloody drunkard than smoking those atrocious cigars, Sutton." Tom ignored him.

The next morning, Tom was up by 6 am. He had washed and was dressed in a navy suit, tie, crisp white shirt, and shiny black leather shoes. His hair was combed and slicked back, and he was clean-shaven. The image of an upstanding gentleman was complete and softened by the sling resting on his right arm, a gentle reminder of the injury that had brought them here to start with. Weasel had risen early, too, and was looking well groomed, in his own Weasel kind of way. He quickly rubbed his shoes with a handkerchief to give them a quick shine before the two friends left the flat in search of Wilkinson's office.

Staring at the grand iron sign "Wilkinson and Atkins," Tom pounded the lion-faced knocker with his free hand. The two men shifted their feet as they waited for a response. A minute later, the heavy door opened, and a wizened old man welcomed them with a gleaming smile.

"Please come in. I am glad you could make it, Mr. Sutton. Oh, and you too, Mr. Byrne, we have been expecting you."

Weasel and Tom exchanged glances and then followed the amiable chap into the large foyer dominated by a thick mahogany staircase. The old man led them to the office door to the left of the staircase labeled *Wilkinson*, which promptly opened as they approached, and the same bald man Weasel had encountered at the train station a month earlier stood before them, a large grin extending from ear to ear.

"Ah, Thomas Sutton," said the man extending his hand eagerly. "And Mr. Byrne, of course," he said with a slight frown.

"What makes you think I am Thomas Sutton?"

"Because you fit the description Mr. Van Wyk left me exactly. And besides, I have already made the acquaintance of your colleague here, Mr. Byrne. Isn't that right, Mr. Byrne?

Weasel scowled slightly at the man but nodded in agreement. "Please do come in and make yourself comfortable," said the man motioning to the two large armchairs on the other side of his desk. He was definitely of British origin, betrayed by an accent that he had not chosen to not quite acclimated to this place, and that alone put Sutton on edge. Tom and Weasel took their seats, and from across his desk, Wilkinson lifted the lid of his cigar box and offered it to his guests. Tom softened and graciously took one of the cigars while Weasel waved his hand in dissent and glared at Tom.

"I take an immediate liking to a man who appreciates the finer things in life, Mr. Sutton," said Wilkinson as he leaned over the desk to light Tom's cigar before lighting his own and relaxing back into his chair opposite the two men.

"Thank you," said Tom leaning back in his chair with a momentary air of importance intended for Weasel.

Wilkinson looked straight through Tom's piercing blue eyes and raised his eyebrows in a challenge.

"I suppose you are wondering why I have asked you here, Mr. Sutton?"

"Yes, we are both intrigued, aren't we, Weasel?" said Tom acknowledging his friend in the mystery.

"I have been waiting for you for some time. I had begun to worry that you would not come."

Wilkinson rested his cigar in the amber crystal ashtray on his desk and reached down and pulled out a file from his desk's side drawer. He sat up straight in his seat and cleared his throat as if he was about to deliver a dissertation. He pulled a sealed envelope from the file and placed it on the desk before Tom. Tom glanced at the envelope, which read "Mr. Thomas Sutton" in an eloquent hand, and exchanged a quizzical look with Weasel.

"Mr. H. C. Van Wyk placed this envelope in my care before his death, with the intention that it makes it into your hands, Mr.

Sutton. However, before I can allow you to read the letter Mr. Sutton, per my client's instructions, I must ask you a singular question.

"Ask away," said Tom casually.

"It's not quite that easy, Mr. Sutton. I will need you to place your right hand on this bible, please, and swear an oath that you will answer this question honestly and if it is affirmative, that you will see it through to the best of your ability."

Tom creased his forehead at this unusual request, and his mind shifted back for a moment to the last time he saw the Dutchman, wondering what he could have kept so secret. He had had ample time to share his thoughts with him as he languished in his bed those many months ago.

"What is this all about?" Tom said carefully

"Do you, Mr. Sutton, intend on taking this oath?" said Wilkinson seriously

"I do," Tom said honestly with direct eye contact.

Tom swallowed the lump in his throat, and Wilkinson placed the Bible before him and retrieved his forgotten cigar, and took a long puff. Sutton placed his hand on it and waited for the question.

"Repeat after me, please."

"Do you, Mr. Thomas Sutton, wish to adopt one Heidi Van Wyk?"

All of Tom's emotions collided. What could the Dutchman possibly mean? Adopt his daughter? Didn't he know, when he was alive that Tom had cared for Heidi like his own child? Why hadn't he spoken of this then? What was this game he was playing from his grave?

Wilkinson shuffled nervously in his seat and repeated the question, more sternly this time. "Do you, Mr. Sutton, intend to adopt Heidi Van Wyk?"

"Yes, uh, yes…absolutely I do intend to adopt Heidi Van Wyk." Tom said clearly.

"Alright, then, Mr. Sutton," sighed Wilkinson with relief. "You may now open the envelope."

Tom carefully took the envelope and ran his finger over his name on the front, which had been penned by a man no longer in his world. He tore the seal and pulled out the letter. He recognized the hand of his friend Van Wyk and his very tone lifted from the page as if he was sitting beside him.

The Offices of Wilkinson & Atkins, In the presence of T, Wilkinson Esq., July 2nd, 1923

Dear Mr. Sutton, I hope I may now call you Tom.

By the time you receive this, I will no longer be by the side of my beautiful Heidi. I pray that my child does not mourn my demise for longer than God demands. If you are reading this, you have accepted to adopt Heidi under oath, as I instructed Mr. Wilkinson. Please forgive me for the formality, but this is my child and treasure, and I needed to make sure that your intentions were true and unobstructed before we continue.

I am truly grateful that I had the opportunity not only to meet you but also to observe you with my child in the short time we had together. I was able to contemplate your honesty and friendship not with me alone but with my daughter. In a way, I am grateful to have you read this letter after my death so you are left with no choice but to listen without interrupting. I saw how broken you were when you first met Heidi. I shared a common heartbreak with you in the loss of our wives, and I came to find that your heart had been broken twice with the loss of your son. It pained me that I could not spare Heidi the heartbreak of losing both parents. I could see that she filled a void in your heart, and I knew that soon she would need someone to fill the void in hers.

I could not find the words to ask this of you before my death, and I did not want her adoption to be entangled with her inheritance. This is why I found it necessary to have these legal assurances, and I hope, as a father, you can understand.

With this letter, you will find enclosed the deed to my twenty-five-thousand-acre property - the farm that Heidi spoke of so proudly in Northern Rhodesia.

You are now the rightful owner, with half the share in Heidi's name, which she is to inherit fully upon her twenty-first birthday. You will find that cattle farming is quite profitable, and with your adaptability and hard work, you can elevate the business further. I have no doubt that you will make a comfortable life for yourself and Heidi.

As Heidi's natural father, I hope you will grant me the following requests:

1. As we are both aware, Heidi is an intelligent, industrious girl. It is my wish that she receives a quality education that will prepare her for whatever pursuit she chooses. I have recommended a school, and Mr. Wilkinson can provide you with further details.

2. I wish to be clear that neither I, nor my daughter shall object if you choose to remarry. Heidi never really knew her mother, and I feel that a mother figure would be of benefit to Heidi to provide her with a female role model. I only ask that should you remarry you take Heidi's interests into consideration and choose someone who would treat her with love and kindness like her own child.

In closing, I hope that you forgive me for the secrecy and method by which you had to hear my true intentions. I needed to ensure that your objectives were not only true but long-lasting. From my heart, I give you my eternal gratitude Tom. I know there are no words or compensation that capture the monumental responsibility required to adopt a child and raise her as your own.

I can finally rest at peace, knowing that my sweet Heidi is in your care. Be true to my daughter, Tom, for I know she will always be true to you.

Yours Sincerely,
H. C. Van Wyk

Tom folded the letter methodically and placed it back in the envelope. He wiped his eyes as they filled with tears. The Dutchman's presence felt so close, as if he were speaking the words over his shoulder. He looked up at Wilkinson and said deliberately.

"He was indeed a wise man, that Dutchman. I shall never forget him. And I promise to keep his memory alive for his daughter." He passed the letter to Weasel to read for himself.

"Indeed, Mr. Sutton. I am glad to see his wishes finally come to fruition. I have the legal adoption papers here for you to sign. They are already filled out…just need your signature."

Wilkinson presented Tom with the documents, and, smiling at Weasel, whose eyes were a bit wet too, Tom signed it gladly.

"Here is the deed to the property, along with Mr. Van Wyk's recommendations for Heidi's education. I will gather any additional information and other incidentals on the property and have those ready for you to pick up before you leave Cape Town."

"Thank you," said Tom. "Mr. Wilkinson, I cannot express how glad I am that you sought me out. You have changed two lives today... actually three," he said, looking at Weasel with affection.

"There is nothing more exhilarating than seeing a dead man's final wish satisfied." Mr. Wilkinson said with relief. "Now go and get your daughter Mr. Sutton."

CHAPTER 2

PART 1: THE TREK NORTH TO MOSI-OA-TUNYA

With the Dutchman's letter in hand and official adoption papers signed, Tom needed no further validation to prove his rightful guardianship. Heidi was also relieved that she didn't have to spin any wild stories to Mrs. Koning about Tom's worthiness. To be sure, even the administrator was happy for Heidi and the promise of a future for the girl outside the walls of the orphanage.

Beaming from ear to ear with her tiny palm clenched firmly in Tom's, Heidi left her sadness and orphan status behind as they exited the building. Knowing that her future had her father's blessing made this all the sweeter. And even though she'd have to wait, what better place to keep her father's memory alive than back on her farm, where she knew she'd always feel his presence.

They spent a lovely Christmas in Johannesburg, followed by Heidi's ninth birthday on January 2nd. Heidi was spoiled with gifts and confections the likes she hadn't seen since before her father became ill. But she loved the book her Uncle Tom gave her the best. He had chosen Peter Pan because he said it reminded him of his son Sean, and that's why she treasured it. She hoped that, as his daughter, she could somehow help fill the void left by the loss of his son. This book made her feel closer to him than she had ever felt before, and she hoped over time, he might tell her more about Sean and Sean's mother, even though Heidi knew that these subjects were delicate and that adults needed more time to process their grief than children. Not that she was finished grieving her father and mother's deaths, but she had learned how to move forward and be satisfied that they were in heaven, where they no longer felt the pain.

The sheer bliss of the trio's Christmas reunion and her birthday celebration quickly faded in the new year as Weasel and Tom made their plans to return to the Swede and his mine for a final season. They had to honor the agreement that they had signed, especially after all the expenses they had incurred over the last two months.

Tom and Weasel felt it was only right to leave things on good terms with their employer. Besides, if he was going to be running a farm now, he expected he'd need some working capital to get everything off the ground. All his research on farming wouldn't be for naught after all, and he was committed to seizing this second chance that Van Wyk had given him, not just for Heidi, but for himself and Weasel too.

True to his word, Tom enrolled Heidi for the first term at the boarding school in Bulawayo as per her father's request. He had to make special arrangements for her to remain for part of the first term holidays so that he and Weasel could fulfill their contract. Heidi was obviously disappointed that they would be separated again, but she understood the reasons, and this time, she knew that they were inextricably bonded forever. They now officially belonged together.

Heidi knew that quality education was something her father had intended for her, and she was bound to honor that request. And she liked learning, Tom and Weasel reminded her as they escorted her, teary-eyed, onto the train dressed in her smart new school uniform, reminding her at least three times to use the writing set and stamps Weasel had bought her for Christmas to keep them updated every week until they could be together again.

The Swede welcomed Tom and Weasel back with enthusiasm. Although he was disappointed to hear that they would be moving on after the completion of the contract, he was genuinely happy for Tom and Weasel and this new chapter in their lives. He had never had a family, even though he was sure his lifestyle wasn't conducive to one, but his heart warmed at the thought of Tom raising a young orphan girl after losing his own son. Tom was especially sad to see that Simalala had left to return to his homeland. He had hoped that he could have properly thanked the man for saving his life.

Tom put in extra time and worked exhaustedly in those ensuing months to garnish as much cash as possible. By the time Heidi's term was due to end, he had accumulated seven hundred pounds, and with Weasel's contribution, he estimated that they would have quite a good start.

On their last day, Tom and Weasel packed up their few belongings, said their goodbyes to the men at the mine, and then paid the Swede one last visit before they set out for Bulawayo. The Swede pulled out three Castle beers and a cigar for himself and Tom. They talked like old friends about the last year in the mines and contemplated their collective futures. Before Tom and Weasel took their final leave, the Swede opened that elusive safe and pulled an envelope from it.

"This is for you both. I never had the chance at a family and expect I never will. I wish you a happy future with your new daughter Tom. You deserve some happiness."

The envelope held a hundred and fifty pounds. They thanked the man profusely for his generosity and promised to stay in touch. And with a tinge of sadness, they bid adieu to the Swede, who continued to wave until they were mere specks on the horizon.

Heidi was elated and brimming with stories and idle chatter when they arrived at the boarding school to collect her. Tom met the headmaster, who seemed like a reasonable gentleman, even though he was a touch too pompous for Tom's liking. Perhaps it was his British tone that irked Tom. But in general, he was impressed with the place. The grounds were neatly manicured, and the rest of the staff in residence seemed friendly and accommodating. The other students he encountered seemed happy and engaged. Best of all, Heidi looked well. Her cheeks were flushed, and her hair glistened like gold in the sun, neatly braided in a long plait. She seemed content and somehow more grown up than when they had seen her last.

"It's all the rules, Uncle Tom." Heidi explained, "We are taught to behave like young ladies, maybe that's why I seem more grown up to you."

"Now they can't be taking the sprite out of this lass," Weasel said with a wink, and Heidi had to laugh.

Heidi said goodbye to some of her new friends with warm embraces and giggles that one would expect from a gaggle of nine- and ten-year-old girls. This helped reassure Tom that he had made the right decision enrolling her here.

As they left Bulawayo, the train took a slight jerk before its wheel reeled against the hefty metal tracks, the engine exhaling thick clouds of burning charcoal against the expansive blue sky. Pressing her nose to the window, Heidi watched Bulawayo fade into the horizon and exclaimed excitedly.

"We are finally moving, Uncle Tom. I won't have to go back to school until next term."

"Hey, I thought you liked your new school? What about all your friends?" Tom said, poking fun at her.

"Of course, I like my new school, and I will miss my friends. But I have waited so long to go home and to be going home with you, Uncle Tom, and you too, Uncle Timothy."

"And so, you have!" Tom said sincerely.

"Well, I will tell you one thing," Heidi announced histrionically. "I can't wait to get out of these threads," she said seriously, and both men laughed until their sides hurt.

Heidi stood up with her hands on her hips and modeled her green tunic dress, matching beret, and black patent shoes to further laughter. Her yellow plait, tied with a green bow, swung across the middle of her back.

"No hats or shoes required on the farm," Heidi stated, making her point.

"Soon, your hair will be longer than the tail of a Palomino Pony," exclaimed Tom

"What is a Palomino Pony, Uncle Tom?"

"It's a horse, Heidi," Weasel interjected with a smile.

"Not a flaming horse," Heidi gleamed proudly at Weasel, earning his grin in return.

"Heidi!" Tom reprimanded

"Sorry, Uncle Tom. I meant to ask what kind of a horse is a Palomino?"

Heidi batted her eyelashes apologetically at her uncle, pecking his cheek. An antic that she had perfected as far back as the boarding house. She realized how quickly a simple gesture of affection worked like a charm to deescalate almost any situation.

"It's an American horse that has the same color mane and as your hair, Heidi," Tom said laughing

"I was about to tell her that," Weasel remarked, earning a sly grin from his friend and Heidi.

Heidi tossed her beret on the seat and swung her braid from side-to-side, whinnying like a pony as the two men laughed at the sight of her. Their banter had not gone unnoticed by the other passengers, who continued to stare in their direction. Ignoring the gazes boring into his back, Tom was relishing every minute of their reunion and refused to allow strangers to taint these moments with his ward.

The trio continued to laugh as Heidi imitated every farm animal that they would soon meet, complete with chirping and grunting noises. Their euphoria was rudely interrupted by a plump arrogant woman wearing a ridiculously large hat.

"Little lady, had your mother been here, she would have objected to you being such a public nuisance."

Heidi's demeanor became suddenly solemn, and she turned to face the woman staring straight into her eyes and stated unapologetically, "My mother is dead."

Tom and Weasel stared at Heidi with pride. Any other child would have sought the shelter of an adult, their parent. But it became clear to Tom at that moment that part of Heidi's precociousness and confidence had simply come from a place of self-preservation. She had been alone in this world for a while now and had been forced to be her own advocate, much like he had as a child. At that moment, he had overwhelming respect for the little girl, but at the same time felt sad to think that, like himself, she had been forced to grow up before her time.

"Well, then your father here needs to take disciplinary action!" continued the angry passenger.

Heidi didn't waver but held her ground and met the woman's anger head-on. "My father passed away too. This is my Uncle Tom."

This time Tom intervened. Heidi was his child now, and he swore to himself that he would take this burden of advocacy from her so that she could be a child again.

"Madam, I suggest you poke your large hat into someone else's business and take a seat. My daughter here has had enough of you for one day."

Flustered by the confrontation with Tom, she waddled herself back to the rear of the carriage, bumping several passengers with her imposing hat on the way to her seat. Heidi wrapped her arms around Tom, and tears filled her eyes. No words were spoken, but Tom knew that from that point on, Heidi understood that he was always in her corner, and she would no longer be alone to fend for herself.

Heidi settled herself back in her seat, and holding her hand, Tom turned the conversation back to the farm.

"So, tell me, Heidi, what do you miss most about the farm?"

"Oh, Uncle Tom. I cannot even tell you how delightful it is to be going back. I cannot wait for the train to get there, so I can show you my home, I mean our home. We have lots of mango trees…do you like mangoes? Tom nodded. "And all the animals, of course, and the servants will be running to get everything ready, so we won't have much cleaning to do. I love you, Uncle Tom."

"I love you too, Heidi."

"And you too, Uncle Weasel," Heidi added, to which Weasel tipped his cap.

Tom placed his arm around her little frame protectively as she leaned against his side and closed her eyes to rest. Weasel had begun to slump in his seat opposite them, and before long, his friend appeared to have dozed off too. Tom allowed his lids to get heavy, and together with the two people in the world that meant the most to him within arm's reach, he drifted off.

As the Victoria Falls Bridge approached, Heidi woke Tom and Weasel, jumping up and pointing in her seat. It was like she could feel home was close, and her yearning couldn't contain her excitement any longer. They all moved to the left side of the train carriage and pressed their faces to the windows, becoming lost in a communal trance as they approached this marvel of modern engineering. Heidi had made this trip many times, but it never lost its thrill. Tom and Weasel had heard tales of the famous bridge and Livingstone's Victoria Falls or Mosi-oa-Tunya, as it was known by the natives.

David Livingstone, a Scottish missionary and explorer, came upon the Falls in 1855 and renamed it in devotion to Queen Victoria. But to the natives of this land, it would always remain Mosi-oa-Tunya, "The Smoke that Thunders," and it did indeed thunder. The two men had never seen anything like it.

The bridge had been the conception of Cecile Rhodes. It was part of a plan to connect the Cape to Cairo by railway, which never ultimately materialized. And although he had died before construction on the bridge began, the bridge had been completed some twenty years earlier, spanning the Zambezi River and effectively connecting Northern and Southern Rhodesia. In his vision, Rhodes had wanted train passengers to not only see the natural wonder up close but to feel the spray of the Falls in passing.

As the train inched closer to the bridge and the Falls came into sight, Tom and Weasel stared in awe at the natural brilliance before them as Heidi squealed in delight, thrilled to show them her Mosi-oa-Tunya. The Zambezi River gushed and plunged over 350ft into the enormous 5600 ft wide gorge below, and as the train moved onto the bridge, they had a front-seat view. It was a sight the two men could not fathom. They were mesmerized by the grandeur before them. The nobility of the majestic Zambezi River, glistening in the noonday sun appeared both refreshing and simultaneously terrifying. The vastness of the Falls was breathtaking, and the adults remained glued to the window even as the train screeched to a halt on the other side.

Heidi, meanwhile, had already gathered her school things and had even managed to change out of her school uniform and into her homebound dungarees and checkered blue shirt. It wasn't until they heard the conductor that Weasel and Tom turned to find Heidi waiting at the exit, ready to disembark.

Now that the rainy season was over, the temperature lay comfortably around 77 degrees Fahrenheit. The men had expected a temperate journey ahead of them, but as they disembarked the train, they were affronted by stifling humidity conjured by the Falls before them. The men exchanged a look and together removed their dress shirts, tying them around their waists.

They had promised Heidi all the way from Bulawayo that they would get off at the Falls and explore for a few minutes and then make their way to Livingstone on foot. So before disembarking, Tom asked the conductor to please take their luggage on to Livingstone Station so that they could get off and look around a bit. The conductor gave Tom a curious look at the suggestion but assured them that he would have their luggage stowed at Livingstone station, awaiting further instructions.

Dressed in undershirts, slacks, and suspenders, Tom and Weasel followed Heidi off the train. Much to Tom's chagrin, Heidi had also removed her shoes and socks and insisted on traveling barefoot.

A hundred yards in the distance, a familiar dark figure emerged, sitting on the side of the road with a large bundle on his head. Recognizing them, he quickly rose and rushed to meet them.

"Simalala!!!" cried Tom as the two men collided in an embrace. "Your arm good now, Bwana Tom?" Simalala remarked

"Thanks to your Simalala. Thanks to you!" he said, slapping the man on the shoulder.

Weasel then stepped in and vigorously shook the man's hand. "You big bastard! What are you doing here? When we asked the Swede where you were, he just told us that you had gone back to your people."

"I come home. I no work in mines no more. I sit here to rest before I walk to Livingstone, six miles left now."

"Six miles!" said Weasel exhaustedly. "Are you bloody serious? I thought the Livingstone Station was just over the bridge?"

The two men exchanged a frown and turned to face their little navigator, who was now shifting sheepishly from one foot to another. Tom leaned down and questioned her.

"Young lady, you said that the town of Livingstone was on the other side of the bridge, now I find it's six miles away? No wonder the conductor thought I was daft."

The traveler's bellowing laughter caught them off-guard, and the three of them turned back to Simalala. "Six miles is not so long. Maybe she's not been to Mosi-oa-Tunya in many years."

"Young lady, you are not out of trouble yet," Tom said, half scolding, half laughing.

"Simalala, this troublemaker here is Heidi." "She's your mtwana[1], Bwana Tom? Your child?" "Yes, she is my daughter."

Tom smiled at Heidi. At the word, Heidi threw her arms around Tom's waist, and all was forgiven.

"She is not a troublemaker. Your mtwana is a moneymaker. She will be sold for many cattle as the labola when she marries and will make you rich."

This was the traditional custom of this land, and Simalala stated it indifferently as Tom and Weasel exchanged a quizzical look, deciding it was best to change the subject.

"Why don't you come with us, Simalala?" Tom asked.

"You allow me to walk with you, Bwana Tom?" Simalala said, who wasn't used to terms of equality between Africans and white men.

"It would be my honor, Simalala." Tom beamed at the man, whose eyes glistened with respect for him.

As they continued their journey, Heidi occupied herself conversing with Simalala in Lozi.[2]

---

[1]   Child
[2]   Barotse Language

Weasel whispered in disbelief, "Wonderful, now she can speak some African lingo. What bloody next?"

In retaliation, Tom started speaking Gaelic to Weasel as they walked ceremoniously past Simalala and Heidi. The girl wasn't upset but intrigued by this strange tongue, which she had heard them devolve into before, and jumped to Tom's side, begging to learn more.

"Why should I tell you what we were saying when you are busy speaking in some African dialect?"

"Please, Uncle Tom, please!"

"Young lady, it is bad manners to be communicating in a language that other members of the present company do not understand."

"I am sorry, Uncle Tom. I promise I won't do it again. It's only that I grew up speaking Lozi before I really even spoke English. And you were also speaking to Uncle Weasel in Irish?" she reprimanded gently.

"I was speaking in Gaelic. And I was telling Weasel about how I know this little girl who is about to be punished for bad manners," he said with a grin on his face.

"I'll teach you Lozi if you teach me Gaelic Uncle Tom," Heidi said precociously as she pranced on ahead of them all, singing distinctively in English.

"Why were you walking alone, Simalala?" Tom asked as Simalala caught up with them again.

"I was to meet my brother before we went to Mombova and then go North to the land of my people. But he never comes, so I need to go to Livingstone to find him."

"Then let's go to Livingstone together."

"Today, I go to Livingstone with you. One day, you will come to my land. I wish for you to come there." Tom heartily agreed.

Moving past a cropping of trees, a birds-eye view of the Falls came into view, forcing the small group to stop momentarily and take in the expanse. The rage of the river free-falling off the peak from this angle was stunning.

"It's pretty, Uncle Tom, isn't it?" said Heidi smiling wide, placing her left hand on her forehead to shelter her eyes from the sun rays that glistened off the water.

"Smoke will come after the Zambezi is in full flood." Simalala intervened as he exhaled, dropping his shoulders and adjusting the bundle of his belongings on his head. Tom looked at the man with confusion.

"The mist, Uncle Tom. He means the mist." "What mist, Heidi?"

"Floods that build up when the river flows over Mosi-oa-Tunya," answered Simalala proudly.

"After the rainfall, the Zambezi is in flood for hundreds of miles, and as the river races to the sea, millions of gallons of water can be heard and seen thundering over Victoria Falls. That causes a mist to rise so high that we can see it from our farm. The Africans call the mist "smoke," Heidi elaborated boastfully. This is why the Africans call it Mosi-oa-Tunya. The mist from the water looks like smoke, and the sound of the river thunders. So mosi that thunders." Heid said eloquently.

"Ah, the Smoke That Thunders," Tom repeated. "Now I understand." The all stood in silence for a moment and then resumed their journey.

"Oh, I wish the waterfall was mine, Uncle Tom."

"My Heidi, it is yours and mine and Weasel's and Simalala's. It belongs to everyone who falls in love with it. It's a gift from God," he said, patting her affectionately on the head.

Moving away from the Falls, they continued to walk along the dusty roadway toward Livingstone. An hour into their journey, Simalala and Heidi remained unfazed by the humidity, but it had begun to wear on the Irishmen, who decided to rest for a moment under a sparse tree that provided little shade. Not that a sliver of shade would help in this humidity anyway. Weasel squinted, making out the outline of a scotch cart in the distance behind them. He convinced Tom to rest there until it approached, hopeful that they might secure a ride.

A cacophony of barking reached them before the cart was in clear view, causing them all to rise. The cart was pulled by two musk oxen, secured with a thick leather harness, and led by a small African boy that couldn't have been more than six. A corpulent woman sat on her throne, a worn-out old armchair, with her trusty blunderbuss strapped to her left thigh at the ready. Her white skin was parched, and the shadows from her hat created a look of stubble on her chin. The cart stopped, and she screamed something indistinguishable to shut up the six mangy dogs who yapped incessantly behind her before addressing them. Her voice was hard and masculine, and she spoke in a thick Afrikaans accent.

"Rooinecks[3]. Can't take the heat, eh?"

"It is rather toasty, Ma'am," Tom muttered, perplexed by the sight of the woman.

The woman laughed loudly and robustly, cracking her whip at the dust near their feet.

"Well, get on board, Rooinecks, unless you wish to perish in the heat. It won't be cool till night."

Obliging her generosity before she changed her mind, Tom lifted Heidi into the cart, and the two Irishmen piled in. No one uttered a word. Weasel was especially disconcerted and sat as far from the oversized woman and her pack of dogs as possible. Simalala trailed on foot behind them, recognizing that the driver would not take kindly to offering him a ride as well. Tom objected, but Simalala simply put his finger to his lips in a sign of silence and smiled. The cart rolled on towards Livingstone for some time before the woman broke the silence.

"I missed your name, mind repeating yourself, sonny?"

"Oh, I'm sorry, Ma'am, I never introduced myself," Tom stated flatly.

"Not very courteous of you." She sneered in her manly voice.

Ignoring the woman's irksome manner, Tom introduced himself and Weasel.

---

[3]   Redneck

"And the girl?" she said nosily.

"Heidi, Madam. She is my niece, and I am her guardian since her parents have passed away."

"So, where are you headed off to, Sonny?" "A farm called Demberra[4]."

"Was that not the property of Van Wyk? Met him a few times, he wasn't a bad old Boer. I heard about his passing."

"He was my father," Heidi chirped proudly.

"Come sit up here with me, my dear," said the woman patting the seat next to her as if she was going to eat Heidi for supper. Tom reassured Heidi, and she joined the woman.

The woman continued to barrage Tom with a wide range of questions over her left shoulder. He successfully dodged them with short, succinct responses while exchanging knowing glances with Weasel across the cart. Even Simalala seemed to understand the awkwardness between them and offered them an expression of solidarity.

She was quick to pass her verdict against Englishmen when Tom informed her of their Irish heritage, and he was grateful that he fell on the right side of her favor.

"You will have to teach these Irish Rooinecks, my dear," she bellowed as she pulled Heidi firmly against her plump sweaty frame as Tom looked on apologetically.

As soon as the oxen began to trek uphill toward Livingstone, the woman loosened her grip on Heidi, who slithered back to her uncle's side, relieved to be free of the woman's large, perspiring body. Honoring Tom's request, the woman dropped them at the station, and the trio swiftly exited the cart, grateful for the ride and silently more grateful to be free of the woman. Her rowdy dogs started barking again, and she silenced them with a lash from her sjambok[1,] which narrowly missed Tom's head as he slipped off the back of the cart.

"Demberra, you said, sonny? I'll swing by sometime."

---

[4]   Mountain

"Thank you for the ride, madam," Tom said as they all groaned internally. He managed to plaster on a smile and waved at her until the scotch cart disappeared.

Weasel sighed loudly and uttered the first words he had said since they had accepted the ride.

"Please don't visit!" What a bizarre woman, and what a collection of mongrels," Tom signed, making Heidi giggle and even Simalala crack a grin as he comfortably rejoined their group. They stopped in at the station to make sure their luggage was stored and to ask where they could spend the night. They had intended to make at least an overnight stop here in Livingstone to break up the trip, pick up a few supplies and see the capital.

Leaving the station, the odd little group continued into the town as the sun beat down on them relentlessly.

"Where are we going, Uncle Tom."

"To the Northwestern Hotel, at least, that was the station master's recommendation."

Heidi piped up proudly, recalling a place from her past, "I know that place, Uncle Timothy. That is where Papa and I used to stay."

"Well, the young lady, then please lead the way. I believe we could all use a cold drink." Tom announced.

As they walked on, Simalala hung back and suggested that he would seek an alternative route. Puzzled as to why the man would refuse the offer of a cold beer after their long walk, Tom asked why.

"It's not allowed in white people's place. So, now I go see my brother in his hut. The last time I saw him was four years ago."

Tom bowed his head in understanding, "But you promise to come and see us before you leave. The place by Kabi Siding on the tracks north of here?"

"Yes, I come to Demberra in four nights before I go to my people."

Simalala didn't look back, but the trio watched the bobbing bundle on his head take the path to the left and dwindle out of sight. Heidi looked curiously at Tom and Weasel. In her short life with her father in Northern Rhodesia, she had never seen white men interact with African men as equals. This type of friendship was just not customary, and she found it curious.

"Uncle Tom, why were you talking to the Muntu[5] like friends?"
"Because he is another man, and he is my friend, not just a Muntu, Heidi."

Heidi crossed her arms to answer Tom as if he was the child who needed to be instructed on the customs of this new land.

"But Uncle Tom, here you don't talk to Munts like they're friends."

"Well, I do, young lady. Because to me, he is a man just like Weasel and me. If Simalala had not been there for me that day in the mine, I would not be alive, and you, my dear, would have no future. Do you understand?" Tom said sternly as he walked on ahead with Weasel, leaving Heidi to trail behind, contemplating what he'd said.

Heidi was immediately ashamed. She was intelligent enough to follow Tom's logic and question the ideology she had grown up with in white society.

It seemed to her that Uncle Tom's way of thinking was more in line with the biblical teachings that she knew, like the back of her hand. *"For the Lord, your God is God of gods and Lord of all, the great God mighty and awesome who shows no partiality and accepts no bribes"* - Deuteronomy. Or the famous passage from the gospel of Mark *"You shall love your neighbor as yourself. There is no other commandment greater than these."*

She sped up to catch up with them and gripped Tom's large palm with both of her tiny ones and pressed her cheek against it in an apology so heartfelt that Tom stopped and bent down on one knee to face her.

"I am sorry, Uncle Tom. If he is your friend, then he is my friend too."

"It's alright, child, you have a lot to learn. We all do."

Tom kissed her on the head, smiling at her humility and desire to change.

---

5   African

Weasel interrupted, whining, "What about me? What about the beer you promised, Tom? What about you leading the way, Heidi? Don't you care for your Uncle Timothy, who is losing weight by the second in this Turkish bath?"

Heidi and Tom laughed, and walking between them, holding both their hands, Heidi led the way to the hotel as they swung her wildly every few steps to giggles.

The Northwestern was indeed a landmark in the town and was bustling with white locals. Wide red brick steps approached the long verandah which spanned the front of the hotel. Upon arriving, Weasel was the quickest to settle into a large chair at the farthest end of the verandah, directly under one of the large ceiling fans that churned a cooling breeze over the area. Tom flopped down next to him, grateful to take a break from the blazing sun and dusty road, as they salivated, waiting for a waiter to find them.

Heidi walked around the verandah as the men chatted, absorbing all the familiarity. She remembered exactly where her father used to sit and the stories he would impart as she sat wide-eyed, sipping her ice-cold Coca-Cola from the bottle. She was exhilarated to be back in her hometown and on her way to Demberra, where she belonged.

CHAPTER 3

PART 2: THE TREK NORTH-LIVINGSTONE

It didn't take Tom and Weasel long to begin to doze off under the cool drone of the overhead fan, weary from their journey. When someone nearby cleared his throat, Tom opened one eye to see a lanky waiter smiling at him. He was an older man, evidenced by his graying hair, and he was dressed in a starched white shirt, which stood in direct contrast to his deep dark skin. He stood a few feet away, tray in hand and pad at the ready.

"Would you like to order something, Bwana?"

"Oh, yes, sorry. Two Castle beers and a Coca-Cola for this *mtwana.*"

The waiter scribbled down their order and, with a nod, retreated to the bar, throwing a smile at Heidi as he exited. As Tom watched the waiter leave, another man entered the verandah. He was stout and white, with well-weathered tanned skin, and dressed in a battered-bush hat, long khaki shorts, and a short-sleeved cuffed khaki shirt. His trousers were pulled up over his protruding belly, and the thick white socks he had stretched over his large calf muscles made him seem shorter and rounder. Removing his hat, he revealed a full head of gray hair and inquisitive beady, light, brown eyes. He made his way toward the newcomers.

"Good afternoon, gentlemen. I hope you're having a nice day in this humid little town. I gather you must know by now that Livingstone is a tourist hot spot. Excepting the occasional game hunter, we aren't used to seeing strangers like you here in these parts. Allow me to introduce myself and extend my assistance to you. I am Leonard Johnston. And you are?"

He was clearly British, and immediately Tom and Weasel were wary. But Tom rose, dusted off his hand, and extended it congenially. Weasel followed suit.

"I am Thomas, and this is my friend, Timothy. And gesturing to Heidi, who stood politely with her arms grasped behind her back like a proper schoolgirl, he introduced her as well. "And this is Heidi."

"It's nice to see you again, Mr. Johnston," said Heidi sweetly, and then became quickly distracted as her Coca-Cola arrived on the table beside her. Weasel and Tom exchanged looks.

After the formalities, the men settled back into their chairs as the waiter deposited two ice-cold beers before them. "May I offer you a beer Mr. Johnston" offered Tom hospitably.

"No, my dear man, thank you, I have had my quota for the day. But I will sit for a moment if you don't mind."

And without waiting for an invitation, Johnston took the vacant seat next to them, and the farthest from Heidi, who had now taken out her sketchbook, was busying herself, seemingly uninterested by the men to her left and their conversation.

"So, the daughter of H.C Van Wyk?" "The one and only, Mr. Johnston."

"Please, there is no need for the formality. You can call me Len. Everyone else does in this town." He looked over at Heidi for a moment.

"Do you know how similar her hair is…or should I say was… to Charles' in his younger days. Quintessentially Dutch, wouldn't you say?"

At the mention of her father, Heidi looked up, and Len offered her a sad smile from across the room.

"It was tragic to hear about his death. He was a good man… a friend. I felt sorry for the little girl when the news finally reached us. But who would have ever thought his daughter would return? So, you're an acquaintance of H.C.'s Tom?"

Tom took notice of his speculative and inquisitive tone. He was fishing, so Tom retorted.

"Caretaker and legal guardian of Heidi and her father's ranch from now on, Len."

Len disguised his surprise quite well. "Such a relief to hear that, Tom. We could use a new wave of energy to brighten up this place."

The waiter returned like clockwork with two more ice-cold beers as if he had anticipated their thirst. They quickly drained their first ones as he placed two fresh ones before them, removing their empty bottles with a nod.

"Ah, what the hell, bring me another Samson," said Len dismissingly to the waiter as Tom and Weasel exchanged looks. "Ah well, one more couldn't hurt," laughed Len explaining his change of heart.

They discovered that Len and The Dutchman had been quite close and had been regulars at this establishment. Without divulging his tragic past, Tom explained how they had met the Dutchman and how the man had deemed him worthy enough to adopt his daughter upon his death. For his part, Len was happy to give him the lay of the land and tips on where to buy supplies. He seemed like a nice enough chap.

Weasel spoke very little and just clenched the perspiring bottle of beer and sipped away. Heidi glanced over and smiled at Weasel, who winked back.

"When are you heading to Van Wyk's farm then, Tom?" "We thought we might spend a night here in Livingstone and acclimate ourselves. Our trunks are being held at the Livingstone Train Station until we are ready to leave."

"So Kabi Siding is your stop."

"That's what we have been told…on the route to Lusaka."

Tom relaxed back into his chair and pulled a cigar from his shirt pocket, lit it, and exhaled a puff of rich tobacco smoke into the air around them. Len ignored the smoke and settled into his cordial, which had been placed on the table in front of him, while Weasel turned his head to avoid the insipid smoke with a grunt of disgust.

"You don't have to worry about that, Tom. Len said congenially, "Allow me to arrange for your luggage. I'll have the station-master ensure that it's loaded onto the train for you whenever you are ready to leave. This way you can relax here for a couple of days. Get to know the town. You might even spend some time buying clothes suited to the weather, or else I fear your friend here could suffer from heatstroke." Len smirked, raising his glass to Weasel, who toasted him half-heartedly.

Tom squinted his eyebrows and looked down at his own attire. Even though they had put their shirts back on, his long trousers and cotton shirt rolled to the elbows were quite moist with perspiration and clearly unsuitable for the weather. He had to chuckle to himself as he imagined Weasel's skimpy legs in shorts. He was only able to suppress his laughter when his eyes settled on Len's bulky hairy legs protruding out from his shorts.

"I suppose you're right, Len, we will need new digs," said Tom snapping his suspender.

"And when you're ready to leave, Tom. I'll have the train stop right here for you three. Just let me know the day."

"Here? In the middle of a town? Is there a station nearby?" asked Tom, dumfounded

Len waved away the question in a flourish. "No, not at all. But I can have a station made right here, especially for our new arrivals. Look, see, the railway tracks are a mere fifty yards away," he said, pointing to the tracks visible from the verandah.

This was highly irregular, thought Tom and Weasel, but they decided to ignore their skepticism for the time being. In time that they would learn how this town worked. For now, they were grateful for the help. Although there was much to see in Livingstone, and Heidi was excited to show them around, Tom was anxious to not delay their journey by more than a day. And he was still a bit apprehensive about the legitimacy of the "personal" train stop. So, they finished their drinks and agreed to meet the following afternoon.

After they said their goodbyes, Heidi clutched Tom's hand, with her schoolbag strapped across her body, and led the way to all the suitable garment markets in Livingstone, highlighting sights as they followed her enthusiastic lead. Her grin lasted all day as she tugged the two grown men about the town.

After an afternoon of shopping, they returned to the Northwestern, where they checked into a comfortable, tastefully decorated hotel room with two beds and a canvas cot for Heidi. The cot reminded Heidi of the many nights she slept in one, just like it, on hunting trips with her father. She remembered lying very still from the comfort of her cot, her eyes wide open. The crackle of the fire combined with the low, undistinguishable din of grown-up conversation while a symphony of crickets made bush music all around them. There was no combination of sounds Heidi liked better, she decided, and she longed to hear them again. They all bathed before dinner, entirely necessary after a day of sweat and dust. They had a civilized meal of sauté of beef, jacket potatoes, and savoy cabbage in the dining room and retired gratefully, each of them falling into an easy slumber.

They woke the next morning, and after a hearty breakfast and lively conversation, the trio explored the town a little more. Livingstone was still a young town. Originally called the "old Drift," a mere settlement twenty years before, it had recently been named the capital of Northern Rhodesia. In that short time, the town had erected the Northwestern and established St. Andrews Church. Mopani Clark, one of the first Old Drift settlers, had built a central bar and store. In recent years, residential dwellings had popped up, and several little stores, including a chemist, now anchored the capital. Tom liked the newness of Livingstone and expected that it would become a frequent sojourn on their trips back and forth to Heidi's boarding school.

As they returned to the Northwestern around 2 pm, they spied Len luxuriating on the verandah. Tom and Weasel now understood why Len sported a potbelly that protruded between the gaps in his shirt buttons. Seeing them approach, he heaved himself from his chair, draining the last of his drink, and called to them jovially.

"I hope you are finished with your shopping, gentlemen. The train will be here in twenty minutes; I have spoken to the station master, and your baggage has been transferred to one of the carriages, so you'll have everything with you when you arrive."

"Thank you for all your help. How about a drink before we leave, Len?"

"I'm afraid I am no longer a civilian, Tom. One is my limit on workdays. Now I have to act like the exemplary sergeant that I am." he said with a more serious tone.

"I beg your pardon… sergeant?"

"Yes, I'm a sergeant. You know… a policeman."

"You're a bobby, a Bow Street Runner?" Weasel exclaimed in shock.

Tom, on the other hand, was unfazed by the revelation, or at least he covered it well. "Well, then, we won't be keeping you. Let's gather up our things, shall we?" said Tom. Weasel laughed awkwardly.

Tom, Weasel, and Heidi collected their things from the hotel clerk and rejoined Len on the verandah. The trio then trailed behind the policeman back into the scorching hot sun, and after a few minutes, as promised, the train appeared before them. The Irishmen looked at each other quizzically while a lean ashy, blond-haired man dressed in a pale blue button-down official-looking shirt and dark blue slacks, jumped from the engine to greet them. Heidi looked up to see Weasel gawking at the sight before him, making her elbow him on the thigh. Tom rolled his eyes at the two of them and shifted his focus to the hushed conversation taking place between Len and the engine driver, Charlie.

"You don't have any proof to take me in, Len."

"Stay watchful, Charlie. I have my eyes on you. It won't be long before I catch you red-handed."

"You'll be hard pressed there, Len?" yelled a ruddy-faced man, the train's fireman Bert, from the handrail that extended from the front of the engine.

Tom and Weasel turned in his direction, and he waved at them affably before jumping down and disappearing around the front of the engine.

Len refocused on Charlie, the engineer. "Another time, Charlie, you hear me! Changing his tone to one more friendly. "But…for now, drop Mr. Sutton and Mr. Byrne at Kabi Siding? The Irishmen here are new to Northern Rhodesia."

"Ah yes, Mr. Sutton, Mr. Byrne, and Miss Heidi Van Wyk, of course."

"Please assist them to the last passenger car before the caboose, they'll find their luggage waiting for them," he said, calling to a train guard who waved to them from the footplate of the passenger car.

Tom and Weasel shook Len's hand in gratitude and walked to the back of the train, with Heidi skipping several feet ahead of them. Tom couldn't shake the exchange between Charlie and Len. Len had been firm, but there had been an air of congeniality between the men as well. Climbing aboard, they all nodded to the old lady who sat in the first seat knitting, a ball of wool trailing down her lap onto the floor in front of her. Their baggage, which only consisted of the men's two canvas steamer trunks and Heidi's very modern leather suitcase, which her father had bought her before they moved to the boarding house, were stowed in the hammocks above them as promised.

Everyone else on the train was well settled in already and either sleeping or reading quietly, seemingly unperturbed by the unconventional train stop. Tom and Weasel smiled and nodded at the passengers that gave them any attention and relaxed into their surprisingly comfortable velvet seats. Heidi, who had already requested the window seat clung onto the window railing in anticipation, nose pressed to the glass. By the time the hiss of steam and the guard's whistle punctured the stillness of the bush around them, Tom and Weasel observed that Len had already returned to his chair on the verandah of the Northwestern only fifty yards away. He appeared to be drinking a coffee. As the hotel dwindled from view and the train trekked north, Weasel and Tom shared the same thought. Was that the only "work" Len would do today?

Heidi, meanwhile, had already left Livingstone behind and was staring northward, hoping to recognize the familiar sights on the ride home. She had been conjuring them in her dreams for the past several months. Despite having traveled these tracks many times before, it had been over a year since she had been home, and she wondered if the land had forgotten her or she had it.

The small oasis of civilization they had left behind soon became a sprawling expanse of African bush dotted with baobab, mopani and flamboyant trees. The landscape was still lush and green from the summer rains. The climate wouldn't change here until May or so when the temperatures cooled, the grasses would become dry and brittle, and Heidi would return to school. Heidi pushed that unpleasant thought from her mind as she strained to remember the landmarks leading her home to Demberra.

"Do you see that farm over there, Uncle Tom? Heidi exclaimed, pointing, "That belongs to Mr. and Mrs. Joshua. They have two Labradors, Susie and Alex."

Every few minutes, Heidi would animate and pronounce the name of a farm as it came into her vision, enlightening her company to what she could remember of the owners. Then she would return to staring out the window as the train clicked rhythmically over the tracks.

"She seems to be really happy to be going back," said Weasel watching Heidi with a smile.

"You would be too if you were returning home," suggested Tom with a slight tinge of remorse. Tom thought better of it and quickly changed the subject, arresting any thoughts of his past and Ireland from this moment.

"Well, Leonard Johnston seemed like a decent man. Funny too. Almost made me overlook the fact that he is English."

"Agreed, although I can't deny that I would love to have his job." Weasel said, "I'm not sure I was cut out for farming or whatever we will be doing at the Dutchman's place."

"I don't know, Weasel. But it's an adventure. You wanted adventure in your life, didn't you, boyo? And we will soon find out what it's all about."

Just then, the guard who had delivered them to their car walked down the aisle scrutinizing every passenger. Tom and Weasel exchanged looks, mildly disturbed by this odd behavior. Seemingly satisfied with what he saw, the man took a seat across from the old lady beneath the emergency cord. Soon the rhythmic pulse of the train got the better of Tom and Weasel, and they began to doze off. No sooner had the men relaxed into a light sleep did Heidi lose her patience with the view. There hadn't been a farm for the last ten miles, and the landscape had become repetitive.

Shaking Tom, she asked pleadingly, "Uncle Tom, can I go to the engine and see how they drive the train."

Slightly groggy, Tom replied dismissively, "What? No, Heidi, the driver would be angry if you disturb him…and young lady, I was trying to sleep."

Ignoring his request for peace, she continued, "but Uncle Tom, I remember Charlie, and he doesn't seem like a person who could be mad. And I wouldn't bother him."

Tom now computing the legitimacy of her request. "Heidi, you cannot expect me to jump off the steps of a moving train, catch up to the engine, and tell him how you want to join the crew for the rest of the journey."

Realizing the foolishness of her request, Heidi retreated, embarrassed, "I am sorry, Uncle Tom. You are right, of course, but it would have been fun, don't you agree?"

"Maybe someday in the future, Heidi. When we become friends with Charlie…maybe on the next trip to Livingstone, he'll let you."

Weasel opened one eye and decided quickly that he wanted no part of this squabble and tipped his hat over his eyes and slipped back into slumber, or at least pretended to. Tom shut his eyes again, and recognizing defeat, Heidi pulled her copy of Peter Pan from her bag and opened to chapter four, *The Flight*. She had read the book many times already, but she especially loved this part. The Darling children were journeying with Peter Pan to Neverland, flying, of course. She was thrilled by the way Peter became a relentless show-off to impress Wendy, and she loved how the Darling children recognized features of the island just from the stories Wendy had spun. She likened their journey to hers as she again peered out the window, hoping to see a familiar sight pass them by. Suddenly, the drone of silence around her was pierced by a loud scream.

"DOWN!" a passenger screamed at the top of their lungs. Weasel woke with a jolt, but before he could take in his surroundings, he was pushed to the floor with Heidi and Tom on top of him. Tom had instinctually reverted to battle mode. He knew the sound of gunshots when he heard them.

"What in the bloody hell was that?" stifled Weasel from the bottom of the pile. "Pardon the language, Heidi."

Heidi was white with fear and barely acknowledged his outburst from her sandwiched position between Tom and Weasel, her copy of Peter Pan dashed to the floor in the aisle before them.

"I don't know, Weasel. But it doesn't sound civil," said Tom raising his head and slowly rising to his feet. He picked up Heidi's book and looked around the cabin for any clues.

Weasel rose and held Heidi's hand tightly. The Irishmen observed that all the other passengers seemed surprisingly unperturbed, and the guard just stood by the emergency cord smiling. The passengers had simply returned to their business, whether it was reading or sleeping. The old knitting lady lowered her needles calmly and called out to them.

"Nothing to fear, young men. They must have shot a buck."

"Shot a buck? What? who's hunting?' Tom said, bewildered. "Agh, they do it all the time," she replied nonchalantly and returned to her needles without a further word on the subject.

Dusting off his shirt, Tom approached the old lady, determined to gather more information.

"Excuse me, but we don't understand. What's going on here?"

"Oh, this is a marvelous stretch for game shooting. Much to Mrs. van Ransburg's dislike, as this is her property. It makes her boiling angry." She smiled as if she thoroughly approved of the enterprise and again returned to her knitting.

Well, there was only one thing for Tom and Weasel to do, and that was investigated. They wasted no time disembarking the train, stopping only to help Heidi to the ground, she had forgotten all about the Darlings in her Peter Pan book and was thrilled to be on to the next life adventure. They walked swiftly to the front of the train as it stood silent and stoic on the tracks.

"How curious, no one is about. Where is everyone? said Tom as they arrived at the engine to find it vacant.

Tom and Weasel instinctively did a sweep of the landscape around them. Nothing. They walked on foot back to the rear of the train. If the old woman was right, Tom surmised the kill would have occurred at least a half a mile back from where the train now stood deserted of its driver. They walked on foot to the back of the train and then followed the track southward for about 900 yards. Beyond a copse of trees, in the distance to the left, Weasel spotted the engine driver and the fireman, along with a handful of passengers handling a reedbuck. Taking in sight, a devious smile grew on Tom's face. He had an idea.

"Watch this Weasel," Tom said, smiling.

"You have been caught in the act red-handed, Charlie," Tom called out to the gang of hunters, walking towards the scene of the crime.

"A copper!" one of the passengers proclaimed in horror, believing Tom to be a man of authority. With that, passengers fled the scene and scampered through the bush haphazardly to return to their train cars before they became the recipients of any punitive action.

Charlie and the fireman looked utterly dejected. They dropped their weapons and hung their heads in shame like schoolchildren. Tom could barely keep a straight face at the sight of them.

"What now?' asked Charlie deflated. "Nothing?" said Tom grinning.

Charlie was confused, but Tom kept up the ruse. He straightened his posture and, with an authoritative tone, ordered the men to remove the dead buck from the sun. Charlie made the fireman, and one of his guards dragged the reedbuck to the train. It seemed that a carriage had already been prepared in advance to transport the dead animal.

"What next?" asked Charlie, still in a state of suspense.

"A price to keep my mouth sealed," Tom said without a flinch.

"State it."

"My girl wants a ride in the engine till Kabi Siding."

Charlie and Bert looked at each other curiously. "That's it?

…yes, yes, of course," said Charlie happily.

Weasel put the man at ease. "He wanted a ride for the child, and you gave him that opportunity, that's all lads. He is not a policeman. You all can unwind your tension now."

"I knew he was not a bobby." called out the fireman as he returned from storing the buck.

Heidi, who had observed this unusual turn of events with much amusement, smiled from ear to ear. How clever was her Uncle Tom, she thought? Tom and Weasel took Heidi to the engine, and Charlie lifted the little girl up gently, the Irishmen following behind. As the journey resumed with a whistle and loud hiss of steam, Charlie and the fireman continued to steal glances at Tom, who stood behind Heidi with a protective arm around her.

After a few moments of silence, Tom began his inquiry. "How do you manage to take an aim from here? And what if I had been a bobby? You should have maintained more precaution."

"The guard signaled with the emergency cord that the carriage was not infested by any officers of the law. As soon as the brakes were engaged, Bert shot"

"Ah!" said Weasel as he and Tom exchanged looks of revelation, now understanding the odd inspection by the guard before the gunshot.

Charlie continued, feeling more comfortable. "This land, all of it, and all of the creatures living here are the property of Mrs. Van Ransburg. She is the most pompous Dutch woman you'll ever meet. Not to mention her half a dozen vicious bloody dogs and the rusty old blunderbuss that she keeps strapped to her fat leg. Unfortunately, my learned colleague over here, on one certain occasion, instead of a sable antelope, shot one of her treasured possessions, an Afrikander bull, turning Len loose on our tails." Charlie glared at the fireman.

"It was unintentional. I have already told you the lighting obscured my vision." complained the firemen.

"Oh, does it matter now? Moving on!" said Charlie irritably.

Tom interjected. "Mrs. Van, eh. That lady you described… was the one who offered us a ride on her scotch cart into Livingstone yesterday morning, and you'll be glad to know that she is still in Livingstone. We all saw her this morning in town before we left, although we avoided her acknowledgment, if you know what I mean." They all laughed. "But now about the aim. I am intrigued how a man can take a shot like that from a moving train?"

"It's a strange thing. You see, Bert here can perch himself on the cowcatcher, and from that spot, his gauge and aim are always precise. He never misses a single target if the train is still moving. But when it stopped, Bert couldn't even shoot at a barn door. It is a mystery."

Tom and Weasel had to laugh at the image of two grown men shooting from the cowcatcher, recklessly jeopardizing their lives for the promise of fresh meat. Before long, all four men in the cabin were laughing loudly as Heidi examined the dials in front of her with awe, happily engaged with being the engineer for this leg of the trip.

"She's Van Wyk's daughter, isn't she?" asked Bert.

"That's right. He passed away a few months ago, as I am sure you heard. Well, I have adopted Heidi, and we are bringing her home."

"Good man Van Wyk. Well, a friend of his is a friend of ours," said Charlie cheerfully and shook hands.

The remainder of the journey was peaceful and uneventful. Long before Kabi Siding came into view, Charlie applied the brake a mile out and slowed the train to a halt. This time it was a respectable stop, unlike the shocking jolt they had experienced the last time.

Charlie jumped off and then lifted Heidi gently to the ground. Tom and Weasel followed. The emergency cord guard met them outside their car with all their baggage and boxes of supplies. The men all shook hands again, and the train personnel returned to the locomotive. With an exhalation of steam and a signature whistle blow, the train heaved away from the trio. The two men turned to see Heidi staring at what was the Dutchman's home poised majestically on the hill above them. The Kimberly brick Dutch revival house looked distinguished and far more grandiose than Tom had anticipated. It boasted two floors, made possible by the gambrel roof, which gave it the look of a barn. Two gabled dormers on the second floor and a portico with columns at the front entrance with a small porch completed the design. The Dutchman had surely intended to pay homage to his homeland with this farmhouse.

Heidi stared up at her home and said wistfully. "Papa's mountain. He used to sit outside on that front porch at sunrise. From there, you could take in the entire farm. Oh, how I missed you, Demberra."

Tom had never dreamed that Van Wyk's farm would be anything like this. He imagined the Dutchman planning out the farm from that vantage point, his kopje, looking out over the flat surrounding bushland. He hoped that somewhere the Dutchman was looking down on them right now. Tom wanted him to know how grateful he was for this gift, this chance to make a new life here. Again, he silently vowed to care for his daughter as long as he lived. Heidi broke the silence when she tossed off her shoes and took off in a full run towards her father's house, churning sand in her wake.

"It's just the way we left it, Uncle Tom and Uncle Timothy. She screamed over her shoulder. "We're back home. Did you hear Demberra? We are home forever!"

CHAPTER 4

THE DUTCHMAN'S FARM

He shielded his eyes against the noonday sun as he surveyed the expansive twenty-five thousand acres from the new verandah of his home. The Dutchman had been right. This spot had the very best views of the land, and there was nothing better than sipping a morning coffee and looking out over this beautiful land to the train tracks beyond. Tom had set straight to work building this large verandah that ran across the entire length of the front of the house. He had meticulously wrapped it in the mosquito net so that he could even sit outside at night and immerse himself in the sounds of the bush with a glass of Jameson and a good cigar.

This verandah had become the hub of Demberra. Every Monday morning, it served as the center of business operations for the farm. Simalala and Tom met here to discuss plans for the coming week and made notes on the progress and setbacks from the week prior. It was from this outlook that Tom paid his laborers every Friday, who had worked tirelessly under Simalala's supervision to bring the farm back and into a new era. From this verandah, Tom would sometimes hand out tokens of European luxuries like soap and sugar to the farmhands as they became available at the market in Livingstone. Soaking in Demberra's revitalization and his own philanthropy, Tom felt almost like a reinvented man. But most of all, he felt proud that he had fulfilled a dead man's wish. He had been true to his daughter, and he had breathed new life back into the Dutchman's homestead.

Heidi also loved the verandah. When she was home from school during the rainy season, she would sit here night after night, entertaining him with stories about her teachers and their quirks. If it wasn't Mrs. Bitmeyer with her crooked teeth and bulbous ankles, Heidi was imitating Mr. Cryer licking egg from his fingers with gluttony while Tom's belly laughed between puffs of his cigar. Over the last few years, Heidi had mastered the uncanny way her headmaster arched a singular eyebrow when he disapproved of some unladylike behavior, and she would use it to her advantage when Tom reprimanded her, only making him devolve into laughter at the thought of the man. Whether they were playing checkers or chess, reading to each other, or just talking, Heidi kept Tom willfully engaged in the antics of her cheeky friends and their misadventures. Waiting to hear the next installment in her saga of teenage frivolity almost made up for their time spent apart.

When Heidi was away at school, Weasel and Tom had spent countless late nights on the verandah reminiscing over their misspent youth. Sometimes they would be joined by Leonard Johnston and other locals who enjoyed the good company and libations. But about a year after they had arrived at Demberra, Weasel's interest in farm life and farm labor especially had waned, and he had begun to seek out new ventures. Even Leonard had noticed Weasel's restlessness and had tried to persuade him time and again to join the police force, much to Weasel's chagrin. Tom had to admit that he enjoyed watching the game of cat and mouse between them, which was especially entertaining after both men had a few too many.

Regardless, Tom understood Weasel's restlessness and bore him no resentment for wanting to leave. In some ways, he had always felt a little guilty that Weasel had been forced to hitchhike onto this new life of his. But he assured Weasel that wherever life took him, Demberra would always be a light in the storm for him whenever he needed it. In the months that followed, Weasel traveled to and from Livingstone and became acquainted with a robust Dutchman commonly known as Mooi Boetie or "pretty boy," a perfect oxymoron for the six-foot-three, pock-faced hunter. He was an odd man of few words who wasn't exceptionally well favored by the locals, but Weasel had taken a liking to him and vice versa, probably because he was a man of few words. When Mooi Boetie asked Weasel to accompany him in the pursuit of ivory, the unrestricted employment appealed to Weasel, and he accepted enthusiastically.

After nearly four years in service to Mooi Boetie, the thrill of hunting, trekking, and sleeping in the bush for weeks at a time began to lose its thrill for Weasel. Tom had been surprised that the Irishman had endured it that long. Now well into his forties, Weasel longed for something more stable and independent. Soliciting a handful of Mooi Boetie's contacts and some of his own, Weasel had recently begun working on his own trading post in Katimo Mulilo, north of Livingstone on the Zambezi River. Now that Weasel was establishing more permanent roots, Tom had hoped he might see more of his friend.

As Tom now surveyed the ranch, well populated with cattle and fertile with hundreds of acres of crops, it was hard to believe that it had been quite barren upon his arrival. The moment he had stepped off the train those years ago and first laid his eyes on Demberra, he had been simultaneously both immensely grateful and immensely daunted. Tom realized immediately that he would need to become a quick study. Neither he nor Weasel had any concrete experience with farming or ranching. What little they could remember from their hapless youth in the Irish countryside was of no use in sub-Saharan Africa, and the books he had read in Cape Town only provided a cursory knowledge but nothing practical. So, within weeks of their arrival at Demberra, Tom had offered Simalala the position of farm manager and overseer. He knew that he needed the help of someone native to help him restore and expand this diamond in the rough that Van Wyk had left him and Heidi. Simalala had enough respect for Tom that he hadn't even bothered asking for more details about the position but had agreed on the spot. Other than the occasional visit to his father and village, Simalala had brought his wives and children to the ranch and made Demberra his home.

Tom solidified this agreement with a lease of one thousand acres of land to Simalala. He wanted Simalala to not only make his home at Demberra but to feel as invested in this venture as he did. The lease allowed Simalala to use the property as his own without the burden of taxes, which Tom knew he could not afford. Simalala could breed his own cattle and manage his property as he saw fit without obligation, under the condition that it did not interfere with his duties at Demberra.

African ownership of the private property to this extent was unheard of in 1920's colonial Africa. In southern Rhodesia, the government, which had no African representation, restricted the sale of the property to black Africans. News of Tom's generosity and ingenuity spread. Simalala, along with his father's help, recruited some of the finest skilled labor from his Lozi village, and soon Demberra was operating like a well-oiled machine. Between Tom's scope and planning acumen, and Simalala's knowledge of farming and management of the new labor force, they divided tasks seamlessly and became a formidable team.

With Heidi away at school most of the year and Weasel away on month-long ventures at a time, Simalala became Tom's only regular companion. But Simalala had a family of his own to mind and his own property to manage, so Tom often found himself alone at night, staring out over the land, just like he was this morning.

From this kopje, Demberra was picturesque. At four thousand feet above sea level, the winds here were pure, unlike the humid waves of exasperation that tormented Livingstone, where the mighty Zambezi ruled the humidity barometer. Below the house, twenty-five thousand acres sprawled out to the railway tracks and beyond to the well-worn Great North Road leading to Livingstone. Since Kabi Siding lay on the only railway line from Livingstone to Lusaka, the passenger train would pass by once a day carrying doctors, teachers, salesmen, traders, and businessmen traveling from Victoria Falls and South Africa to Lusaka, or lately, even further north to the Northern Rhodesian mines of the copper-belt. The cargo train made the journey twice a week carrying goods and equipment or a convoy of live-stock from the southern province to the hungry north.

Before Tom's arrival, Van Wyk's house had been rarely visited except for the occasional emergency or when some dubious voyager decided to get off the train and look around. The Dutchman had been a solitary man mostly and hadn't put Demberra on the map the way that Tom had been able to do in the short six years he had lived here. Tom had seen the necessity of ingratiating himself with his neighbors and some of the locals, with whom he had business or simply liked well enough. Charlie and Bert had become good friends, and they would often stop and visit with him en-route to Lusaka or on their way back to Livingstone when they were running the cargo train. The journey from Lusaka to Kabi Siding was over twelve hours, so the two men enjoyed breaking up their journey with a visit, and Tom was glad for the company. With them came news of the outside world, albeit mostly local gossip. It was just enough, he thought. He appreciated the solitude and isolation of this place, and the railway provided a simple daily reminder that he was still connected to the world outside his little nirvana in the bush.

Demberra's fresh air had helped to heal him. The number of the earth in all its richness, the jacaranda trees with their vibrant violet blossoms, and blood orange sunsets were beyond comparison. After all these years, Tom sometimes struggled to connect to the young Irishman's body he had once inhabited. His past had become some other man's story. Sometimes lying alone in bed at night, he forced himself to cling to the fading memories lest he forgets the wife and son he had loved once so completely. But on days like today, he was grateful that he couldn't fully conjure them. Heidi and Demberra had mended his heart over time, and some days it was better left undisturbed. Tom shook those thoughts loose. This was a glorious day!

Heidi was coming home after six months away at school. He had not seen her since June. She had taken a school-sponsored trip to the coast during her five-day August break and had spent her late September break with her best friend Charlotte and her family in Pretoria. Tom hadn't wanted her to go, but he couldn't decline her request to spend her final holidays with her best friend before Charlotte departed to finish school in Switzerland.

Tom had considered Switzerland for Heidi, too, for a moment and was grateful when Heidi insisted that she would get too homesick if she left Africa.

"Besides, I am about as finished as I'm ever going to be when it comes to manners and decorum." Heidi had insisted with one discerning eyebrow raised.

So, Heidi would move on to the junior college in Salisbury to continue her education in June. Tom's heart could handle this arrangement, and he knew it would have made her father proud.

Simalala's voice broke through his daydream.

"Bwana Tom, you leave for Livingstone today?" Simalala asked, emerging on the steps of the verandah.

"Of course."

"You bring your new car?"

"No, Simalala. Driving the car on that dusty road wrecks the bloody thing. Besides, I have no time to spare. Charlie will be coming soon anyway. I shall go with him by train."

"Sure, Bwana Tom. They have cut wide fire guards today, and all is in place. No worry for you."

"Tell them to continue looking out for fires and these fire starters. Our cattle are growing, and we cannot afford to lose a single blade of grass."

"Bwana Tom, you do more than anyone. The farm has thousands of mombies (cows) and hundreds of pohos (bulls). We have more than a hundred calves this year. No one has this many cattle. And you grow more than twenty villages of maize in three hundred acres of your land."

"But Simalala, these are challenging times, and we must stay ahead of the pack. We must continue to work hard and make sure the ranch can sustain everyone here, especially now. Demberra is all we have!"

"You make no sense to me, Bwana Tom."

"I know I'm hard to understand sometimes, Simalala," said Tom laughing despite himself and patting Simalala on the shoulder.

It was 1930, and Africa was not immune to the ripples of the Great Depression, and Tom was concerned about their collective livelihood, something Simalala could not see.

Their conversation was abruptly interrupted by the shrilling whistle of the cargo train as it pierced the tranquil space around them. Gray smoke in the distance seeped slowly into the unpolluted air, making both Simalala and Tom squint their eyes in the direction of the rails as the train screeched to a grinding halt at the siding.

Charlie and Bert waved enthusiastically in Tom's direction, for no one could see clearly through the smoke. Tom watched as they jumped out of their compartment and climbed on board a scotch cart that was commanded by a small African boy that Tom had stationed at the bottom of the hill for their passage. As the cart began its approach, Tom continued his discussion with Simalala, assigning him to check the barbed wire fences to ensure no snares were in place since the calves were roaming freely about the ranch. Losing even one calf to one of those malevolently placed game traps would incur a loss that Tom would not tolerate.

"Oh, and Simalala, make sure Heidi's pony is brought up to the house, to the new stable, when we return… Monday, at noon," said Tom with excitement.

It had been Heidi's greatest wish to own one since she first heard about palominos on the train ride home to Demberra six years ago. It had become every birthday and Christmas request thereafter. Heidi had been taking horse riding lessons at boarding school on the weekends, and she bled Tom's ear dry about it in letters and in person. It had proved more difficult than Tom thought to get his hands on a young palomino pony that was already broken, but he had finally succeeded, and he couldn't wait to see her face.

Simalala shared some of Tom's excitement as he, too, had witnessed Heidi's begging and pleading. He assured Tom that he would make sure the stable boy had the pony groomed, saddled up, and ready for her when they arrived home in three days. He then nodded and departed, leaving Tom to greet his approaching visitors.

As they disembarked the scotch cart, Tom walked down to meet them, cupping his mouth as he called back up to the house.

"Jonas, get the coffee brewing and some steak and eggs, please. The steamer Bwanas are here."

A wave and muffled affirmation came from the kitchen window in response, as if the cook had already anticipated the request.

"Hello, Tom."

"Hey Charlie, how's it going?"

It always confounded Tom how easily Charlie and Bert could abandon their train carelessly at Kabi Siding. This would never have been tolerated across the Atlantic, he thought, but who did they really have to answer to here in the middle of the bush.

At least twice a month, this had become their ritual, especially when Tom had to travel to Livingstone for business or to pick up or drop off Heidi at her school in Bulawayo. They would stop the cargo train right below Demberra and pay Tom a short visit. Drinks and food were always parred for the course, and Tom was happy to indulge them.

As the train's fireman enthusiastically shook hands with Tom, Tom asked.

"What's your score now, Bert?"

"Oh, don't ask, Tom," said Bert dropping his shoulders sadly. "I'm afraid my hands have lost their mastery. Besides, all the restrictions and setups make it harder than before. There just isn't any freedom anymore, I tell ya."

"Damn straight! It's just not as convenient as it used to be. Everything has a price tag now. Not like the good old days when we could fire off a couple of rifle shots and have free meals for a week. How little do we get for putting up with these civil servants. Always intruding, these nasty little white pricks scribbling down about everything in sight, just to have their report glorified somewhere in some report or newspaper." sneered Charlie.

"And there is too much train traffic on board these days, too," interjected Bert. "So much so that you cannot even take a quick stop any more from Choma to Livingstone to take a dump, or they'll be writing crap in their diaries."

"No pun intended," laughed Tom, tickled by their disdain for progress and protocol.

Tom spoke a silent word of gratitude that he had been little affected by the Depression, while Charlie continued to rant about Northern Rhodesia being infiltrated by the foreigners who were doing little to their claims of bringing progress to the land. Living off the land had had its benefits, thought Tom, but he also feared some of the changes he had seen over the last year.

Desiring to maintain his positive mood Tom shrugged it off and consoled Charlie with a slap on the back.

"Ah, don't be too mad about it, Charlie. I assure you this shall work out in your favor too. Just give it some time. This Depression shall go away just like all bad things do, and your pockets will again be clinking once more. Can I at least furnish you with a hot meal to quell your tempers?"

Charlie nodded, and all three men laughed and started up towards the verandah.

"I don't know, Tom; I fear Bert, and I just cannot digest this domesticated beef you nurture. All these years of sourcing meat from the wilds has tainted our palate with its mark," smirked Charlie as they ascended the verandah, where a steaming pot of hot coffee awaited them on the sideboard.

Now that they were moving into their rainy season, the heat wasn't as debilitating as it had been the month before. To combat the warmer months, Tom had improvised an awning with bougainvillea that clung loosely to a wood frame erected against the exterior of the house. After six years, the vines were now robust, and together, they created a flowering canopy against the whitewashed façade. The delicate pink flowers, which nearly bloomed year-round in the lush soil at Demberra, fluttered in the breeze like rustling tissue paper.

Six modern English-style white wicker chairs graced the right side of the veranda, complemented with orange cushions that matched the mustard oche floor that Tom had varnished to help keep the space cool. A round art deco-style iron table and four matching chairs were set for three on the left of the verandah, next to the sideboard. Two low tables locally handcrafted from the bark of Mukwa trees served as coffee tables for the wicker chairs. The ivory tusk over the door and sizable Kudo and Sable skulls hung ceremoniously above them, claiming the space as undoubtedly African.

Charlie admired the recent upgrade of mosquito netting as he pulled a chair from the dining table and plopped down, wiping the sweat from his brow. It was much cooler under the shade of the verandah. Bert joined him, pulling off his cap and tossing it underfoot.

Jonas emerged, wheeling a cart with hot food from the kitchen. While Tom helped himself to a large mug of hot coffee, Jonas placed a loaf of bread, a bowl of curled butter, fresh papaya, and a jar of jam at the center of the table and plates of fried eggs and steaks in front of Bert and Charlie.

The men declined the hot coffee as they usually did at first, and Tom poured them each a scotch from his finest bottle, as was their preference. For their own good and for the train's welfare, Tom had Jonas discreetly abscond the bottle when he returned the cart to the kitchen before the men could partake in another. They would have to follow scotch with coffee thereafter.

"Yeah, I just cleaned it up a bit. Nothing drastic," said Tom modestly as the men surveyed the newly varnished floor.

Tom settled for a slice of bread and jam and some papaya as they chatted. He was too nervous and excited to eat. Besides, a steak would sit in him like a rock and not serve him well on the day ahead of him. Bert and Charlie prattled on about the local gossip in town. Much of their conversation had little substance and consisted mostly of hearsay, second-hand accounts of local drunkenness, and leud extramarital rumors, peppered with the occasional run-in with the law. It was only when they began to speak to the impact of the government's land restrictions, as they had observed by train, that Tom's ears really perked up.

To help increase their influence between South Africa and Kenya, the British government encouraged white settlement in the north by reserving land for white ownership only along the railway line route. African reserves had been marked out around those areas for native blacks. Tom had already heard about this from Simalala, and as conditions had worsened this year, Tom had encouraged Simalala to have the laborers and their families move to Demberra, where the food was plentiful, and space wasn't a commodity.

The men corroborated Simalala's story. The African reserve lands had become overcrowded, leading to food shortages and soil exhaustion from overuse. According to Bert and Charlie, few whites were taking advantage of this prime land reserved only for white settlers because, as Tom suspected, everyone's eyes were fixed on the copper mines in the north and not on farming.

"A bloody typical British move," said Tom with exasperation. "They've always been such a greedy lot."

"That's the truth," said Charlie. "But don't let Johnston hear you say that. It's every man for himself." he laughed with a tinge of sadness.

Charlie and Bert wiped their plates clean, and after a second cup of coffee, the men were ready to get back to the train, and so was Tom. Tom called to Jonas with instructions for a while, he was away and grabbed his bush hat, jacket, and the small suitcase he had stashed under the sideboard.

"Ready?" Tom said, eyeing the men enthusiastically.

"Let's go," said Bert rising and wiping his hands off on his striped company-issued slacks and retrieving his cap. Charlie grabbed a slice of bread for the journey and wrapped it in his handkerchief.

"You know how much I love Jonah's bread," he said apologetically.

"Take the whole loaf," said Tom generously "it won't last until Heidi and I get back anyway." As Charlie wrapped the remaining loaf in his handkerchief and they left the verandah to climb back on board the scotch cart, it struck Tom at that moment how nonchalant he had become about food. No matter how bad this Depression had become, that was the one thing that remained stable on a farm. He had forgotten that that wasn't true for so many.

As the men climbed aboard the awaiting scotch cart for the journey downhill, Tom asked curiously, "Could you imagine if you had passengers and you two abandoned your train for these long breaks?"

"We'd never hear the end of it, that's why we only do this when we have the cargo run. That is unless you want to serve breakfast to fifty people?" Tom laughed.

"Besides, the guard is very vigilant," said Bert. "He's taken his position rather seriously in his caboose. Funny story, yesterday, we nearly lost the bugger. He was trying to take a piss from the door while the train was moving up a steep slope. We lost him, and we didn't even realize it until we were in Livingstone and searching like hounds for the man."

"Luckily, he landed in a grassy patch," said Charlie, and they all laughed.

Tom realized why he liked Bert and Charlie so much. They reminded him of the comradery he used to share with his mates in Ireland, easy and full of silly banter and dumb jokes. He missed them.

As they dismounted the scotch cart, Tom gave the African boy a couple of coins and asked the men as they climbed aboard the engine.

"I hope you two won't be hunting today. I don't want to get into Livingstone too late."

"What's the anticipation, Tom?"

"Well, Charlie, today is Heidi's last day of boarding school. I'll be staying at the Northwestern tonight in Livingstone as usual, but I want to be up and out bright and early tomorrow morning so that I can get to Bulawayo on time for her commencement.

"Now I understand the urgency…no hunting stops planned! Finishing standard school already. Boy, where has the time gone?" said Bert earnestly.

"I know. I can't believe it, either. I bought her a pony, you know. I am also going to treat her to a fancy dinner to celebrate tomorrow night, now that she's a young lady. So, I've reserved a table for dinner and a room at the Selbourne. Then we'll head back to Livingstone on

Sunday and home on Monday. And then after the Christmas holidays, she's off to the junior college at the university in Cape Town in January, where she will complete her studies."

"You must be very proud of your girl Tom. And you've done right by her," said Charlie. "I remember the first time you rode this train with Heidi to Demberra. Remember how enthusiastic she was to be up here with us driving the train."

"That's one way to put it." laughed Bert

"She's still all that Bert…full of energy and completely headstrong," smiled Tom proudly.

"Haven't really seen much of her lately, have we, Bert?" added Charlie.

"Well, boys, you know how young girls can be, it's an awkward age. Besides, you must admit that it isn't easy trying to have a conversation with you two on a normal day, and worse still with other passengers about, especially when you're holding up the train," explained Tom as the men shrugged in agreement.

Bert was right, though, that first trip seemed like a lifetime ago, thought Tom. And it was true that Bert and Charlie had witnessed fewer glimpses of Heidi over the past few years. When Heidi was home from school, and the men stopped the train to visit with Tom during the week, she was typically afoot on the farm somewhere, and their interactions with her amounted to hellos and goodbyes. Tom suspected that as Heidi got older, she had started to feel uncomfortable in adult company, especially men's company. It was easy when she was a little girl, but now he guessed that she was unsure of her place in society. Was she a child or an adult? Around him, she was still happy to be her chatty, silly self, and he was grateful for that, but it wasn't so easy for her around other men.

Charlie and Bert usually refrained from weekend visits with Tom at his request when Heidi was home from school out of respect for the little time that they had together. And although they saw Tom and Heidi four times a year, at least as she traveled back and forth to school, those interactions had been similarly insubstantial.

Raising a young woman was something Tom had never expected to do in his life, and he found the whole conversation about her growing up rather awkward. Tom became quiet and leaned against the compartment divider beside Bert as they watched Charlie tug the lever making the train shake and rattle against the tracks. The whistle blew loudly, and Demberra became a hazy image in a cloud of smoke as the train pressed on.

As soon as they were underway to a familiar clickety clackety drone, Charlie broke the silence.

"Little Heidi must be all grown up now, Tom? It's been quite a few months since she's been home, right?"

"Yes, she's turning sixteen right after Christmas," said Tom swallowing the lump in his throat, hoping that the conversation might navigate elsewhere.

"Soon enough, you'll be having a hard time with all the young men who'll come knocking," said Charlie with a grin.

Tom creased his forehead for a moment and looked at Charlie sharply, making Bert drop his shovel as reality dawned on him.

"Oh, I wouldn't want to be the poor bugger that falls for your Heidi." laughed Bert.

Tom scowled as Charlie and Bert continued to tease him about the variety of ways he might torture the multitude of young men who would seek to whisk Heidi away. Then they laughed at how Tom would have to endure his future role as father-in-law to some wanton scoundrel. Tom had to laugh with them, but his mind began to wander. He had to admit that he had tried to deny the fact that Heidi was growing up, mostly for selfish reasons. He didn't want to think of her as anything more than a helpless eight-year-old girl with a bowl of soup who desperately needed him.

He had also turned forty last month, and if Heidi was going to get herself all grown up to leave him for some lechetous scoundrel as Bert and Charlie had proposed, what would she do then. Grow old alone? None of it sounded any good.

He was happily thrust back to reality when Charlie suddenly put on the brakes and pulled the train into the next loop, stopping abruptly at the red light. He shook his head as the vibration of another train heading north thundered past them on the only existing track. Charlie and Bert bellowed out loud a string of profanities while the other driver mouthed a few of his own, emphasized by an angry fist raised in mid-air at Charlie.

"Dear Lord, what is old Henry mad about now?" said Bert nonchalantly, although everyone knew why Henry was so angry.

"Man, he's always mad about one thing or another," stated Charlie, matter of fact.

"Maybe, it's because you had him waiting in the loop down the track at the next siding for nearly an hour now, Charlie," said Tom stating the obvious, while the other men chuckled like schoolboys.

They loved to torment the old driver on account of his easy way with Johnston. Bert and Charlie had long suspected that it was because of old Henry that they had to watch their backs with the law, as it pertained to their extracurricular hunting.

"That's right… no green light for that old bugger until we are tucked safely here in the loop that's the rules!" said Charlie definitively as if to say, "I'll show him who's in charge."

The comfortable conversation returned like a well-worn glove for the remainder of the journey and the four hours to Livingstone passed in no time, thankfully without any further discussion with Heidi. Charlie bypassed Livingstone station and dropped him right in front of The Northwestern, as had become customary. Tom stepped off the train and was instantly engulfed by the all-too-familiar humidity that defined this town.

As Tom waved and the train crawled southward to the Falls, he felt a pang of anticipation. Anticipation, excitement, exhilaration, and a little fear combined just as they had that day six years ago when the little band of three had seen the first glimpse of the mighty Victoria Falls from the train window. That same feeling beat in his chest as Tom stood staring after the train and watching it diminish from view. Why did this feel like this was a new chapter, he thought, and why was he feeling so uncertain about the future? Was this Depression finally getting under his skin, or was it the anticipation of Heidi returning home grown up and different, or was it a combination of the two. Maybe it was just the excitement about his gift for Heidi, he decided. Pulling a cigar from his breast pocket, he pursed it between his lips, lit it, and took a long drag expunging the nagging emotions from his body as he turned to face the Northwestern.

Much had changed since June. The once-animated town had become stagnant and lifeless. Bustling market stores had been boarded up, and only the local general store and chemist remained open for business out of sheer necessity. There was an eeriness to the barren landscape devoid of travelers and locals alike. It was true then, Tom thought. The impact of the Depression on the mines and even commercial agriculture forced migration out of the cities because they could no longer sustain an economy. Again, he felt grateful that he was not among the agricultural set that had been forced into bankruptcy, and he knew some good people who had.

He allowed himself a moment of hubris that he had been able to sustain himself, Heidi, and even his laborers and their families through this downturn and that, against the odds, he had been able to grow and expand Demberra despite the economic challenges. He exhaled a ring of smoke full of gratefulness and relief.

Even the Northwestern, which had always been the epicenter of the town, looked mostly deserted save for a finely dressed young couple, who looked distinctly American dining on the verandah, probably tourist explorers, Tom thought, and a familiar round-bellied patron affixed to his usual armchair staring in Tom's direction. Tom waved at Leonard Johnston, and taking one last draw, he dropped his cigar, tamped it into the dirt with his boot, and crossed to the hotel to meet him. The man beamed broadly and placed his mug of beer on the table before him, yanked his bright white socks to his knees, which made Tom laugh to himself, and descended the porch stairs to greet him. He had long since given up any attempts to apprehend Charlie and Bert in their illicit gaming activities, but his due diligence on these local matters had earned him a promotion to an inspector. With crime on the rise, illegal smuggling from the mines, and a waning economy, he took his office more seriously than ever.

Tom found it ironic that he had traveled halfway around the world to rid himself of the British only to form a bond of friendship with a British police officer of all people. But Len was different. He was a local, one of them, and Tom's past was of no consequence to him, not that Tom had been very forthcoming about it either.

"It's been a while, Len?"

"Tom, what a pleasant surprise! How have you been?" said Len shaking his hand vigorously.

"I've been fine myself, just keeping busy with the ranch." "There is talk that Demberra is doing even better these days, despite this Depression. So many farms aren't doing well. I suppose you've heard. It's bloody awful watching this town go to sleep."

As they climbed the steps to the hotel, Samson was ready with a Castle lager for Tom as he took a seat next to Len's honorary armchair. He suspected that Len had ordered it for him when he disembarked the train.

"Thanks, Samson. I've been trying to come to pay you a visit," said Len settling back into his drink. "But I've been so busy trying to track down these smuggling rings."

As Len raised his beer to his lips, Tom noticed how his hand trembled slightly. Len was not aging well. His excessive consumption of alcohol had taken its toll. Tom had been headfirst in the bottle once for a short time, and he knew its lure. Len did somehow manage to compartmentalize his habit, though. When he was on the clock, he was quite industrious and effectual at his job, but Tom knew that this disease would eventually engulf him, and for that, he was sorry.

Len continued in a matter-of-fact tone, "I saw Byrne a couple of weeks back. He was here for some supplies."

"Oh yeah, how was Weasel? I haven't seen him for some time now. At least four months, I think." I got a letter from him a couple of months ago, but he's not the best at writing."

"He's good. Actually, too good," said Len leaning in a little. "What do you mean?" asked Tom, slightly confused by his tone. "Rumor has it that your friend is making quite a fortune. And given that he's barely a trader and no one really has any money right now, you see this place, right? … well, some say he is linked to the Congo gold smuggling ring."

"Weasel? How can you be certain?" uttered Tom with concern.

"I'm not, Tom. I'm not. I'm just sharing with you what my ailing ears have heard, friend to friend. Maybe when you see him next, you can talk to him about this before I do it myself if you catch my meaning."

Tom didn't need to be told twice. This was a warning shot. Len was giving him a head start to extricate Weasel if this was the case, and he was glad for the candor and their friendship. He didn't put it past Weasel to pursue any lucrative endeavor, regardless of the legality. As far as Weasel was concerned, if it didn't hurt anyone, what was the issue. Tom could hear his friend explaining his reasons already. But he couldn't let Len know that.

"I can't believe he would do such a thing, Len. But I will talk to him the next time he comes to Demberra."

"Or maybe you might take a trip to Barotseland. If he's involved and news reaches my superiors, then I will be left with no choice but to pay him a visit." Len said sympathetically. "He should have joined the force with me you know. I could have kept him out of trouble."

Maybe Len was more astute than he thought. "I completely understand, Len," said Tom earnestly. "Thank you for giving me a chance to talk to Weasel first. I understand the stakes."

"Thank you, Tom. So, what brings you here to Livingstone? Off to collect that little troublemaker of yours?" said Len, genuinely glad to change the direction of the conversation.

"That's right. Tomorrow is her commencement from school in Bulawayo. Then she'll be home for Christmas and then off to Salisbury to finish her studies."

Len joined in Tom's pride over Heidi's achievements. He had always liked the child and was happy for some good news during this difficult time. After discussing Heidi and the ranch for some time over another round of drinks, Len graciously accepted Tom's offer to join him for dinner, and the men continued their conversation as Len briefed Tom on all the news from Lusaka to Livingstone and even from the south.

Since the turn of the century, Livingstone has been the gateway to the north of the Zambezi River. Rich in timber and farming, it had become the main supplier to the growing tourist trade in Victoria Falls in Southern Rhodesia. However, due to the Depression, demand for timber had declined, and the tourist trade in the south had taken a blow. Len validated what Bert and Charlie had surmised regarding white settlement and clarified Tom's own prediction that the northern copper mines were to become Rhodesia's future.

Len even went so far as to suspect that Livingstone might eventually lose its status as the capital in favor of Lusaka to be closer to the Copperbelt. They parted ways shortly after 10 pm, with an assurance from Tom that he would reign in his friend and a promise from Len that he wouldn't be a stranger to Demberra.

There was another reason Tom wanted to be up bright and early that Saturday morning. He had one important stop to make before catching the trolley to the train station. Stepping off the verandah, Tom walked south on Mainway. All the official businesses were here on the north end of the town. From the hotel steps, it was a short walk to the bank, post office, British Colonial government building, the hospital, and even Moore's chemist, which were all situated to the west of the hotel within easy walking distance. Behind the business epicenter of the town stood the water pumping machine that supplied water to all of Livingstone's residents and businesses and a small thermal station that was erected in 1906 that provided electricity to much of the town.

Across from the hotel on the other side of the railway tracks lay the police station, quite convenient for Len, Tom thought with amusement. The northeastern part of the town housed the markets and library. Asian and mixed-race businesses occupied the eastern and central portion, while black residential areas, home to local black African tradesmen and servants, covered the southeastern portion.

It was a ten-minute walk to Israel's Bernstein's office, which was situated up the hill next to the post office. From his front window, he could see straight down Mainway, and from the back window, it was not uncommon to view bare-breasted young African Unfazies nursing their babies outside the hospital steps. Israel, or Issy as Tom had come to call him, found this quite distracting.

Tom stood in front of the glass door. *I Berry, Properties bought and sold, Pawnbrokers, Money Lender (when cash is available)* was boldly inscribed on the glass in fancy black lettering. Berry strategically replaced his real surname, Bernstein, so as not to arouse negativity in this predominately white Anglo-Saxon society.

Tom pushed open the door without knocking. Israel, a wiry man of about sixty dressed in a waistcoat and slacks, was seated behind his desk. He had a full head of dark curly hair, dusted with gray and round spectacles that had been pushed precariously to the bridge of his nose. His chair had been turned sideways, and he was staring transfixed out his back window as Tom entered. He jumped with embarrassment at Tom's intrusion while Tom shook his head with mock disapproval and laughed.

Tom liked Issy, especially because he was not British. He was a shrewd businessman, who had steered Tom right since the first time he had stepped into his office over five years ago looking for guidance, and Tom appreciated his brutal honesty.

"So how is business going, Issy?" said Tom with a grin.

"Ugh, so-so," replied Issy recovering quickly from his embarrassment. I have two pieces of news for you; good and bad."

Israel extended his open palm towards Tom without a word. Tom smiled and reached into his breast pocket and retrieved two of his prized cigars, handing one to Issy. Tom relished the opportunity to share his habit with another discerning smoker and leaned across the desk and lit Issy's cigar before igniting his own and settling into the velvet armchair opposite him, reserved for clients.

Exhaling a puff of gray smoke, Tom started, "So let me assume, after our last interaction, that I did not secure the King's place?"

"Not entirely. Though I still can't quite figure out why you are after that damned land in the first place. You are running Demberra at a profit while the rest of the world is crippled."

"Because Issy, it is more land. He has twenty-two thousand acres of fertile land that isn't being used. I can make use of it. More land equals more cattle."

"You don't need the King's place, Thomas, you are doing so well on your own," stated Issy, definitively flicking ash into his ashtray and leaning back in his chair.

"Be out with it, Issy," said Tom suspiciously. Issy never called him Thomas or declined to make a land deal.

Sighing, Issy explained that when Matthias King had passed earlier that month from a run-in with a cape buffalo, his land, instead of going to auction, had passed to James Bradley, a colleague of King's nephew, to settle a debt of some sort. It was all quite hush-hush.

Tom knew of Bradley. By his estimate, he was a nasty young Brit who oozed superiority and had ceremoniously declined Tom's hospitality twice, apparently due to far more important business affairs in South Africa.

"I've approached him, Tom. He's not interested in selling or even leasing."

"Does Bradley not see what I've done with Demberra? He knows how much I need the land with my ranch expanding. He is just being an opportunist. He doesn't care about the land or the people. He's going to ride this out and strike when this is all over. What a bastard!"

"Well, he did say he'd sell under one condition." "What? Spit it out, Issy!"

"Well, I was reluctant to even tell you because I think it would be foolish of you to accept it."

"Go on," said Tom with agitation

"Three thousand pounds for the land," said Issy with another pull of his cigar and a slight cough.

Rising, Tom slammed his fist on the table. "You can't be serious? Where on earth does he think I can get that kind of money from? Or anyone, for that matter-Depression or not. You know almost everything I have is reinvested in Demberra…the cattle, the labor, the machinery…."

"I know, Tom. That's why I didn't even want to mention it. I knew you'd hit the roof. He suggested that over six years, you must have accumulated at least a thousand pounds in cash, and he suggests that the balance can be paid with a mortgage on Demberra, that's inclusive of your cattle, by the way. I even went so far as to suggest that you might entertain a loan from me to make up the difference if he cut the price in half, but he wasn't interested. He wants Demberra Tom, plain and simple."

Tom returned to his seat and took another pull of a cigar. Both men sat in silence for a minute, allowing the cigar smoke to engulf the space between them.

"Why on God's good earth would he want Demberra anyway. He has no interest in farming or owning a ranch. That's clear. He won't even step foot onto my property. He's just too bloody important for all that you know." said Tom sarcastically.

"I don't know, Tom. That's why I hadn't planned on even telling you. His deal is absurd."

"What is the payback time on the mortgage?" "Two years."

"Bastard!"

"You're not telling me anything I don't know." "Well, I accept."

"What!" said Issy, now rising and crushing his cigar into the ashtray. "You are insane, Tom!"

"Look, just have the papers ready and all proceedings worked out, Issy, and tell me where I need to sign?"

"Please, Tom, give this some more thought. In two years, you could end up losing Demberra. These are precarious times we are living in."

"One condition. We wait until after the rainy season. Heidi is coming home for Christmas, as you know. I'm on my way to collect her now from Bulawayo. So have the papers ready for me to sign. I'll be back for them in June when I take them to Salisbury. I'm sure he'll go for that. And don't you worry about me, my friend, I have a plan." said Tom rising. He extinguished his cigar in the ashtray, leaned across the desk, and tapped Issy on the cheek cheerfully. "I'll have Demberra back and King's land before three years is up, you just wait and see."

Issy shook his head in disbelief but rose and shook Tom's hand. "I know there is no talking you out of things when you've made up your mind. I just hope you know what you're doing, Tom."

"You'll see," said Tom smiling. "Oh, and these are for you. Happy Hannukah," Tom said as he drew a small wooden box of fine Cuban cigars from his coat pocket. "Say hello to the missus for me."

"Thank you," said Issy, taking the box graciously. Tom tipped his hat and stepped out of the broker's office, slamming the door behind him, leaving Issy shuffling papers and mumbling in Yiddish to himself.

CHAPTER 5

SOLEIL

eidi's smile could disarm Tom from across a room, and yesterday had been no different. Although she hadn't sprung into his arms this time, her warm embrace in the great hall of Bulawayo's Preparatory School for Girls grounded Tom like only Heidi could do. No matter the time lost between them, they always managed to reconnect like puzzle pieces. But he couldn't deny that she had changed. In their six months apart, Heidi had matured in seemingly indiscernible ways. She looked essentially the same, but she had grown into her figure, leaving behind an awkward adolescence for newfound femininity. Her smile was the same but somehow more refined and not so cheeky. Even the timbre of her voice seemed different and less childlike. However, by the time they had left the commencement and Heidi had cried and giggled her way through goodbyes with all her school chums, Tom had effectively convinced himself that she hadn't changed one bit and that it was all in his mind.

They celebrated with a fancy three-course dinner at the Selbourne that evening permeated with a familiar banter Tom had missed. Heidi expounded on her trip to Polona Beach in Mozambique. Her cheeks flushed red when she tiptoed around the story of some boys that they had met at the beach, quickly changing the subject, which made Tom laugh to himself. She elaborated on the details of her holidays in Pretoria with Charlotte's family, with anecdotes that she could not possibly have animated in her letters. She spoke reems about Charlotte's mother, how elegant she was and how she knew everything about the latest fashion trends.

This made Tom a little jealous because he could never compete in this arena of women's fashion and admittedly had no desire to either. But that didn't seem to bother Heidi. She was excited to tell him all about her new clothes and promised a fashion show when they returned home. He began to wonder if he'd sent her too much spending money and hoped that Charlotte's mother had imparted some wisdom in the spending of it.

Everything seemed almost normal until they retired to their hotel room that evening. Heidi excused herself to the bathroom for an extraordinarily long time, returning in a long silky nightdress and matching robe, hair pinned to the top of her head and face covered in cold cream.

She offered Tom a peck on the cheek and, observing his expression, mumbled, "What? Charlotte's mother said it's always good for young women to moisturize at bedtime. Goodnight!" and with a determinable sigh, she climbed into her bed, turned off her bedside lamp and faced the opposite wall.

Heidi had never been this formal about bedtime. She had never put cream on her face or put her long hair up to go to sleep before, he thought. He stared into the dark room, mumbling to himself and wondering who this imposter was in the other bed. At home, she had often undressed down to her camisole and knickers right in front of him, tossing her garments carelessly on the floor and bouncing into bed with gusto.

Where did she even get that nightgown, he thought, it was far too old for her? Thank God she hadn't chopped her hair off, which was all the rage these days. What other insane notions had Charlotte's mother corrupted her with? he wondered. Why had he ever allowed her to fraternize with that Charlotte girl and her family in the first place, galivanting around Pretoria, spending the money he sent her on useless creams and women's sleepwear. Tom grunted and turned towards the wall, and drifted off to sleep.

To Tom's relief, Heidi seemed more like herself the following day back in Livingstone. They had a familiar dinner at The Northwestern as Tom filled her in on all the changes at the farm and his last visit with Weasel. He also broached his idea about leveraging the farm to purchase King's adjoining land. That night Heidi even abandoned her nighttime cream ritual, which delighted Tom for reasons he couldn't explain, and they talked into the night until they both drifted into a much more comfortable slumber.

The train ride to Kabi Siding was stuffy but uneventful. The train was full of passengers heading to the copper mines. Keeping the train on the schedule was a necessity today, so Bert and Charlie had little time for conversation, although Tom was sure that Charlie threw him a conciliatory nod and wink when he saw them board. His expression fully encompassed the sentiment, *"Poor Tom, future father-in-law to a local scoundrel."*

"Demberra looks better than ever, Uncle Tom," said Heidi, with her face pressed to the window as the train screeched to a halt. "I am so happy to be home," she said, beaming, which made Tom happier than she could fathom.

They waved to Charlie and Bert as the train pressed northward, and without a second wasted, Heidi took off her shoes, threw Tom a cheeky smile, and bounded fervently up the hill to the house, only stopping once to embrace Simalala halfway through her jaunt. This was her sanctuary, a place where she could be herself. There were no rules of society here, just her bare feet, her Uncle Tom, and the land. Tom followed her in the scotch cart with her trunk and their suitcases, stopping at the top to give Simalala instructions on the big surprise.

Heidi waited for Tom impatiently on the verandah. She already had a Coca-Cola in hand and was examining all of Tom's improvements with exuberance when he reached the house.

"Uncle Tom, it really looks wonderful. In fact, I believe Demberra has never looked this good, and I must say you have some swanky taste in furniture." Tom laughed at her casual slang but couldn't deny how good it made him feel to have her approval and praise. The best was yet to come, he thought to himself.

"I'll have your trunk and suitcases brought to your room. Maybe you want to change before I give you a tour of the farm," said Tom hopefully, looking at Heidi's delicate drop waist iridescent green chiffon dress, matching hat, and out-of-place bare feet. Heidi laughed, nodded in agreement, and hurried inside her room.

Even though her room she thought had become quite childish, with its light pink walls and flowery white furniture, it was cozy and thankfully devoid of adult expectations. Part of her had grown tired of all the rules and standards of behavior at boarding school. She was also keenly aware that Tom didn't want her to grow up, and even though it infuriated her that he could not see the young woman that she was becoming, she did relish the lack of expectations. She quickly changed out of her new dress, discarding it on the toy chest below the window. She chose a plain loose cotton shirt from the armoire that used to be Tom's and pulled on her favorite pair of linen trousers, the ones that Tom had reluctantly bought her last year when she complained that she couldn't help him on the farm in a dress. Comfortable again in her own skin, Heidi flopped lazily onto her bed's pink coverlet and propped herself up on one elbow, staring happily out the window at her mango tree, her old friend, the bearer of fruit and harbor of many a good childhood fort. It was good to be home.

Her daydreaming was interrupted by Tom's conscious knock at her bedroom door. Upon entering, he couldn't hide his delight to see her back in her unpretentious farm garb but teased her mercilessly.

"Young lady, don't you think your attire is quite inappropriate for a young woman of your advanced years?"

"Oh, Uncle Tom, it's only you and me here. Who is there to impress? Besides, these are my Demberra threads, you know that." laughed Heidi with conviction and a cheeky smile.

At that moment, whatever awkwardness had existed between them three days ago seemed to have completely dissipated. She was growing up, and that was a reality that Tom had to face sooner or later. This was why this gamble with Demberra, no matter how confident he was of his abilities, was still a gamble, and he needed his partner on board before he could consummate the deal in good conscience. Sitting on the bottom of her bed, he launched into the subject again.

"In all seriousness, Heidi. You are a young woman now. And I need to know what you think of my decision with Bradley, the man who now owns King's place? I have no one else to discuss this with, and Demberra is as much yours as it is mine. Someday it will be yours in its entirety. Do you understand what I am proposing? And you do know that I don't fully understand Bradley's true intentions? I want you to realize that there is some risk here."

Sitting up, Heidi took Tom's hand in hers and looked earnestly into his eyes. "Uncle Tom, you have never led me astray. I trust that you will do what is suitable no matter the risk. You have worked tirelessly to make this ranch prosper, Uncle Tom, and I believe that whatever chances you take, they are done in my best interest and Demberra's. I trust you."

Tom patted her hand reassuringly. "As much as you trust me, Heidi, this is your property as well. I want your blessing before I make any final decisions. This is a huge commitment, and if I fail, you will be affected by it too."

Heidi grabbed Tom by the shoulders and said emphatically and earnestly, "Well then, as your partner, I affirm that you will be able to live up to your end of the deal, Uncle Tom. It is final now, and you have my blessing." And with that, she placed a kiss on his forehead to seal her approval.

"Well, that's that, then partner," said Tom, and he extended his hand and pulled her gently off the bed.

"Come on, then, let's take a ride and tour the ranch so you can see what's changed since you left."

"Ride? What do you mean ride, Uncle Tom?" said Heidi quizzically. Tom's surprise was still elusive.

"You are in for an early sixteenth birthday surprise, Heidi. Grab your boots."

"My boots? Why?"

"Don't ask questions, just grab your boots and follow me." Heidi was completely befuddled, but she did as he asked and retrieved her farm boots and pair of socks and followed.

When they reached the verandah, Tom instructed her to go back through the kitchen and down the side steps to the back right side of the house. Heidi obeyed, and Tom followed her through the kitchen mumbling something to Jonas about dinner as he exited.

"I have been working on this one for the past couple of years," Tom espoused proudly under his breath.

They descended the back hill, and when they reached its foot, Heidi shrieked with unadulterated delight. Before her, next to the bustling one-hundred-yard-wide kraal of neat African huts, sat a modest paddock fenced in perfectly cut Mopani poles. In the paddock stood a golden filly with a meticulously groomed blond mane and warm brown eyes. She bobbed her lovely head up and down as the hefty black stallion by her side turned to look at them nonchalantly. Heidi's hands were over her mouth. She was still in shock. She had never wanted anything in her life as much as this pony.

"That, Heidi, is a Palomino, your sixteenth birthday present. I wanted you to have as much time with her as possible before you leave in June, so I thought I'd give her to you a couple of weeks early. Besides, she is sort of hard to hide. The black one's mine. I call him Blackie." said Tom proudly as Simalala emerged from the stable, a white pearly grin etched across his face from ear to ear. He also knew how much this pony meant to Heidi and was arguably as thrilled as Tom.

Heidi was still in a trance. Slowly she looked from Tom to Simalala and back to Tom. Happy tears rolled down her cheeks, and she threw herself into Tom's arms.

"Thank you, thank you, thank you, Uncle Tom. You have no idea what this means to me. I can't believe it. I can't believe she is real, and she's mine." She took a deep breath.

"I am going to call her Soleil, you know, like the sun." Heidi looked back with adoration at the pony, who was now staring in her direction.

"Well, go and introduce yourself to Soleil," said Tom releasing her from the embrace and giving her a little push towards the paddock.

Heidi slowly approached the fence, speaking gently to the pony as she climbed over the Mopani poles. Tom followed and rested his chin and forearms on the fence, watching the scenario that he had conjured so often in his mind play out in real-time.

Despite her confident, headstrong nature, Heidi was a gentle soul at her core. She was a natural caretaker. She had obviously seen something worthy in him all those years ago and had nurtured him back to life. Tom understood that it was her deep love for this land and for him that bound her to this place, or she would surely be on her way to Switzerland with Charlotte. She had been a good student these past few years, achieving distinction and honors on her school leaving exams. She rarely complained about anything and had been so patient and loyal to him. This was exactly the reward she deserved, he thought. The joy this pony would bring her would last for years, and perhaps in some selfish way, he hoped that the pony would help erase any pangs of regret she might still hold for not going overseas and instead strengthen her reasons for staying.

He watched Heidi stroke the pony's muzzle, face pressed to its mane, eyes closed as if they were already speaking an unspoken language.

He whispered to himself, "I am proud of you, my Heidi. The man who someday has the honor of having your hand will be one lucky fellow indeed. You have made me so happy, and all I want is the best for you."

As the words left his lips, Heidi approached the fence gracefully, leading her pony as if she had done it a hundred times before.

"I really don't know how to thank you, Uncle Tom. No one has ever given me a gift like this. I know how hard it was to find her, and she's perfect. She makes Demberra complete!" Her eyes misted again as she reached across the fence to hug him.

The love affair with her pony didn't fade, and the ensuing months were glorious. Heidi and Tom rode the ranch almost every day when it wasn't raining, checking on crops, surveying the land,

and watching the farm hands corral the livestock. Tom was especially proud of his new potato crop like any paddy would be, and he enlightened Heidi daily on the versatility of potatoes. Tom was not a trained horseman. His experience amounted to a handful of days bareback riding Mr. O'Malley's old mare in the field that abutted the orphanage. So initially, Tom felt peculiar in his khaki trousers and bush hat astride his sixteen-hand stallion.

But Heidi worked with him on his riding acumen, and as his proficiency improved, he had to admit that horseback was an efficient way to assess the day-to-day operations of the property, and he quite enjoyed the "reckless abandon" of riding, as Heidi called it.

As Christmas approached, Tom received news from Issy that Bradley was traveling abroad for Christmas, and he could not expect word until at least February. Tom was grateful for the reprieve while Heidi was home and for the quiet Christmas, they'd share, just the two of them, without business interruptions.

It didn't take long for Heidi's pale city skin to turn a rich golden brown from countless hours in the sun. In the months that followed, her hair became so bleached that it almost matched Soleil's mane in hue. Her mornings were reserved for her pony, whether she trekked the farm with Tom or rode Soleil in the paddock. In the afternoon, she was in the kitchen with Jonas hanging biltong or learning how to make all sorts of fancy cakes and desserts, his specialty. On rainy days they even delved into the international recipe book she had bought on holiday, whipping up new creations that were sometimes a delight and sometimes an utter failure. Rainy day dinners became a crap shoot, but Tom was the perfect gentleman and never complained, even when the meal presented was barely edible, he would simply say, *"Well, that one was not a winner Heidi."* and Jonas would graciously make sandwiches.

In school, Heidi had learned about a "kitchen garden," and after New Year's, she had started vegetable seeds indoors, determined to get a proper vegetable garden installed at Demberra before she left. A couple of months later, when the seedlings were big enough, she etched out a section of the garden outside the kitchen window, which

Simalala staked out for her and surrounded with wire fencing. In it, she systematically planted her cabbage, carrots, tomatoes, eggplants, cucumbers, and French beans. She was so much like him and probably her father too, Tom thought, watching her in the garden, her overalls covered in mud and her hair poking out haphazardly from the braid that hung down her back. She was a hard worker and a self-starter. She was refreshingly unaffected, and she desperately loved this land.

Unlike ranch cattle that gave birth in the lands, like Tom, Heidi relished the thrill of being woken in the early morning hours to witness the birth of the newest pure bread, Hereford Demberra calf, and those first few months in 1931 saw many. Tom would rouse her by flashlight, with hot coffee in a flask, and together they would spend the next several hours in the stable watching the birth and laughing as the awkward little calf tottered on its scrawny legs stumbling its way to its mother's teat. These pure-breed Herefords would enhance the ranch cattle by interbreeding in the years ahead.

The nights were equally enjoyable, and they didn't waste a single one, subconsciously aware that the end of each day brought them closer to Heidi's departure. Intuitively they both realized that this time could never again be replicated, not like this. So, no matter how tired they were, they filled each night with chess and backgammon tournaments, book recitations, and card games. Tom even taught Heidi how to play poker against his better judgment. Every night ended the same way. The fire would die down its coals, and Heidi would stifle the last of several yawns and drag herself to bed after a sleepy goodnight peck on Tom's cheek.

He would remain and smoke a cigar until the last ember went cold, and then he, too, would retreat to his bedroom. In solitary, he would confront his fears of the future and his demons of the past. Staring into the darkness, he reimagined Heidi as a little girl, asleep with a book in his lap and then new images of her as a young woman in a big city all alone. These new worries flooded his mind and tormented him with thoughts he couldn't control. That dread always drove him back to a vision of Van Wyk in his bed dying and Tom struggling to imagine what would become of Heidi if something happened to him. Thoughts of his own demise inevitably ushered in images of Grace and Sean. The dreamy sequence always started in the cottage, full of life and expectation, and devolved into horrific images of rape and death that rocked him to his core. As the images collided, his guilt again overwhelmed him, and for a moment, death seemed like the easy exit. But it was always Heidi's face that brought him back to his room, to the present, and to Demberra. For her, he would journey on because he loved her, and he knew she loved him.

CHAPTER 6

HIDDEN FORTUNES

June 10th arrived before they were quite ready for it. Since breakfast, Heidi had been cloistered in the stable with Soleil, grooming her until her coat and mane shined like her namesake. She had been crying all morning sporadically, wrestling between pangs of sadness for leaving and guilt for the excitement she couldn't deny in the pit of her stomach. Tom had reluctantly loaded Heidi's trunk and suitcase onto the scotch cart and waited on the verandah for her to return from saying her goodbyes, sipping his third cup of coffee and feeling nervous.

When Heidi arrived, she was a picture to behold. She was dressed in a polka dot sunny-yellow drop waist dress. Her sun-bleached hair was pulled into a loose twisted knot at the nape of her neck, disguised as a short hairdo, and she wore a matching yellow cloche hat and a slip of red lipstick. And something new, black mascara accentuated her deep gray/blue eyes, which only made them more piercing against her bronze skin and peachy cheeks. Stocking legs and not-so-high, sensible black heels completed the ensemble.

"Heidi! You never showed me this outfit in your fashion show," said Tom surprised at how mature she looked.

"I know I wanted to surprise you. So, what do you think?" said Heidi biting her lower lip the way she did when she was looking for approval. "I have gloves in my bag."

"Well, I think you look like a fine young woman of academia," said Tom proudly with a wide smile. Heidi dropped her handbag and hugged him as tears began to roll down her cheeks.

"Now promise me that you will take care of Soleil and have one of Simalala's pikaninies (children) ride her every day," said Heidi breathlessly, Tom nodded.

"And make sure that Jonas keeps weeding the garden, or those vegetables won't survive."

"I will," nodded Tom.

"And take care of yourself while I'm gone… I mean, enjoy yourself. Don't be sad. Have company over to visit. Don't be alone all the time, and have some fun."

"Alright," said Tom laughing. "Who is the grown-up here, and who is the child?"

"Alright," said Heidi dabbing her eyes gently with the edge of her gloveless finger so as not to destroy the mascara.

When the train finally approached, they had said everything there was to say. They shared a few minutes of pleasantries with Burt and Charlie, mostly about the horses, while their luggage was stowed and then took their seats in the caboose for the ride to Livingstone. Their easy conversation about the growth of Demberra was punctuated every hour or so with Tom's request to take Heidi all the way to Salisbury. At first, he nonchalantly suggested, then he encouraged more enthusiastically, and then eventually resorted to tales of abduction.

"I thought we were settled on this, Uncle Tom. If I am to be trusted to live at the boarding house in Salisbury and complete my studies as a young woman of academia, as you so aptly put it earlier, then I must be able to travel at least part of this journey alone…for the life lesson. Don't you agree?" said Heidi with a grin. "After all, Charlotte is off to Switzerland on her own, isn't she?"

"Well, she's a year older than you, isn't she?" he said smugly. "Aren't you glad that I'm brighter than my peers?" trumped Heidi with a wink.

"Alright then. All the way to Bulawayo, and then I will say my goodbyes. I don't like it, though. I'll be waiting at the Northwestern for a telegram before I head home." Heidi nodded in compliance.

Before she boarded her sleeper car two days later in Bulawayo, they shared another fine three-course dinner at The Selbourne. It took over twelve hours to get to Salisbury from Bulawayo, so Tom had made sure her train accommodations were comfortable. He implored the conductor no less than four times to ensure that Heidi arrived safely in Salisbury and demanded that he make sure she met her transport to the boarding house. He sealed his request with a pound and five shillings.

When she stepped off the train in Salisbury, she was affronted with a pleasantly cool breeze and a quieter train platform than she had expected. The conductor had been oddly more attentive to her than the other passengers, waiting with her as her trunk and belongings were brought to the platform. He had a quick conversation with the station master, who politely bowed and then came to stand a few feet from Heidi as the train edged on. The station master waited there without a word until her transport arrived. She suspected this was her uncle's doing.

A skinny man in a grey suit and cap introduced himself to her as her official transport to the boarding house, extending a letter from Salisbury Language and Technical School as collateral. She nodded kindly to the station master, who smiled satisfactorily as the man pushed her belongings ahead of him in a trolley to the waiting Chevy parked outside the station. She smiled to herself as she climbed in. This was nothing like Tom's Lancia Lambda Torpedo, and if he were here, he'd be sure to point out all the differences and gloat.

She had been in Salisbury once before with her father, years before. The town had grown up, at least it seemed so from her hazy recollection. Whitewashed government buildings of various heights sprawled haphazardly around town squares. But despite the many wide fronted glass paned modern shops, displaying the most contemporary fashions, and the cute cafés with outdoor verandahs, the town seemed relatively quiet for a weekend. A few people milled in and out of shops while the occasional housewife or house servant tidied up the front of their look-alike red brick houses on the residential streets. The Depression must have had its impact here, she thought sadly. But nonetheless, it was exciting to be in a new town with new people and new places to discover. And it was the perfect time to be a young woman in the 20th century, she decided, as Tom's overprotective farewell rang in her ears.

"Take good care of yourself, Heidi. Don't let those Salisbury gents lurk around you. I don't want to be forced to come and break a couple of arms."

As the red brick boarding house came into view, she smiled and rolled her eyes to herself, whispering, "Dear Uncle Tom, don't you know I'm not a child anymore, stop worrying."

Tom had stood watching the train disappear into the horizon for nearly half an hour before he moved from where his feet were planted. "Dear God, I hope she's safe," he thought nervously. He retreated to the hotel, where he had a double Irish whisky before putting himself to bed. He had no desire to go back to Demberra immediately, especially since it was now devoid of Heidi, so he decided to indulge in a three-day stopover at The Northwestern in Livingstone on his way home. He had received news from Issy the month before, and papers were waiting for him. And perhaps Heidi was right, he did need the company of other people. Heidi's telegram beat him to Livingstone. He was handed the message as soon as he arrived at the hotel.

"SALISBURY WONDERFUL. STOP
BOARDING HOUSE CLEAN. STOP
SAFE AND SOUND. STOP
LOVE, HEIDI

He could finally exhale!

After a trip to Issy's office to sign the mortgage papers on Demberra, Tom returned to the hotel verandah, surprised to see Charlie cooling under the overhead fan instead of Len, which would have been more customary for this time of day.

"So, who's driving the train then?" Tom started, interrupting Charlie's absentminded daydream.

"Oh, Tom," said Charlie jumping to his feet, startled. "It's the rare occasion that I have the day off. They hired a second driver to fill in here and there. Works for me. I'm getting too old for the hustle. What will you be having?"

"The usual."

The waiter promptly returned with a frosty glass of Castle beer.

"You have done well with Demberra, Tom. It's obvious, even from the tracks. The crop expansion, the cattle, and you don't seem to be slowing down any time soon."

"How can I, Charlie? When I have tasted the sweet fruit of expansion." Tom stated proudly but with a tinge of apprehension.

"So, you went through with it. I thought it might have been a figment of your imagination…or at least I'd hoped it was. You better watch him. He can outsmart a jackal if you ask me." Charlie said with concern. But then he smiled. "But knowing you, Tom Sutton, I am sure you must have a plan up your sleeves."

"Thank you for the concern, Charlie. And no, I don't have a plan up my sleeves. I just plan to pay it back in time, that's all."

"How the bloody hell do you reckon you'll do that, Tom, when money is so short?"

"Well, I have planned a trip to see an old friend back in Barotseland next week. I will buy cattle from him and aim to sell them at a decent profit. You see, I can't sell my own cattle as part of that Bradley's conditions. He even has a mortgage on my animals. It would have been easy to pay him with all the recent births and predicted growth of the herd. But I expect he thinks that will tie my hands."

"I don't know if I should be amused or confused," said Charlie quizzically. "Here you are claiming that you can even buy cattle when no one around here can even afford an old plough ox, and in Barotseland, you say?"

Tom laughed deeply. "Oh, relax, Charlie. I am a simple person who conducts straightforward business like anyone else. You see, it's all about credibility, and my credibility with the headmen there is verified. My Kapita[6], Simalala, is the headman's son see. So, despite having once been robbed of his life savings by some white men, he has learned to trust this white man enough to do business with me."

"You know I heard of that; everyone here has. It's been quite a few years now, hasn't it? Tom nodded in agreement sipping his beer.

"And the police still haven't been able to track down the thief or the money, right?"

"I don't think they ever had a decent description of the devil, to begin with, and in the end, weren't those sergeants running around questioning and arresting every white male in sight."

"Including me I'll have you know." said Charlie looking wounded, as Tom laughed at the thought of Charlie in a lineup at the station in front of Len, the inquisitor.

"Yes. What a comical and pitiful time it was. Anyway, I do wish you all the best, Tom. If there is someone who can navigate a deal with the likes of Bradley, then it is you. You've never actually met the man, have you?"

He nodded to the waiter for another beer. "No, I have not, but I appreciate your belief in me, Charlie. I will rise to the occasion to ensure I don't disappoint you and all those who have placed their faith in me." Tom rose and bowed sarcastically.

"No need to be all mawkish about this," said Charlie, half laughing and dismissing his mockery to change the subject. "How is young Heidi? You just dropped her off, right?"

"She is wonderful. In fact, she had just arrived in Salisbury. Got the telegram this morning. I was heading back to Demberra, but you know the protocol. I always stay here for a day or two, so I can catch up on the latest news and share a drink or two with Leonard.

---

[6]   Manager

And besides, I know it will be lonely there without her, and I wasn't quite ready for that, to be honest."

Charlie straightened his posture and allowed the whisky to provide the bravado. "Good thing she is gone for a while. Probably for the best..."

"Why would you say that, Charlie?" said Tom placing down his glass with a little more force than he intended.

"Relax, Tom. I am not implying anything. I've known you and little Heidi for far too long now to be saying anything."

"Then, what are you getting at Charlie?" "You trust me as a friend, right Sutton?"

"I do. So don't beat around the bush. You know I hate that." said Tom leaning in, clearly concerned.

"Look, I've been here for some thirty years now. I know this place better than my own self. There are good people here and some righteous ones too that can be downright wicked with their tongues, and my ears have been listening. Rumor has it that Bradley set it in motion, which is why I said to be careful."

"Be out with it, Charlie!" said Tom, getting irritated.

"You don't have to yell at me, Tom. This is hard for me to be sharing with you. I was angry, too, when I first heard it. It's only because of whisky courage that I'm telling you in the first place. The gist of it is this - He's made some accusations about you and Heidi… sewing doubt you see about your relationship, and there are people around here who believe him 'cuz they don't subscribe to the idea of a forty-year-old man, who's not real kin, sharing a roof with a sixteen-year-old girl."

Tom felt the blood rise to his temples as he curled his fist tightly, causing his knuckles to turn white. He wanted desperately to lash out at this falsehood. But Charlie was only the messenger, and it had taken courage to repeat these baseless claims, knowing it would infuriate Tom. Instead, Tom rose and shook Charlie's hand.

"I almost hit you, Charlie. I'm sorry. Thank you for sharing these rumors with me. And that's all they are baseless ugly rumors, but I don't need to tell you that. You are a good friend. And for the time being, I'm glad too that Heidi is not here to suffer these accusations. I'll be heading home first thing tomorrow morning in light of this. So, I will catch up with you next week on the route. I don't feel much like conversing right now. If you see Len tonight, tell him I said hello." As Tom made his retreat into the hotel, Charlie rose and shouted after him.

"You may beat me to it, Tom. If fate has it, Len might be crossing your path soon enough."

"What do you mean, Charlie?

"I heard that Len's headed to Barotseland this week for some police work. He was grumbling about having to travel in a shoebox-sized boat upstream.

"Hmm. Good to see you, Charlie," said Tom genuinely.

Upstairs, as he turned the key in his hotel room lock, realization dawned on him and made his stomach cease. Leonard had never left town for police work. The most that senior inspector ever traveled was a few miles up and down the railroad track to catch someone red-handed for buck hunting without a license.

"For God's sake, Weasel!" uttered Tom with exasperation as he stood staring at the keyhole.

The next morning Tom stormed out of the hotel toward the railway tracks and the waiting train. Charlie watched sheepishly from the engine, recalling the conversation from the night before, but waving pleasantly as if nothing had happened. Tom tripped on a tuft of bush grass on the way and dusted off his trousers with infuriation.

A well-dressed concealed figure on the other side of the verandah blew a puff of cigarette smoke from under his fedora and then spat in distaste. He had slicked blond hair, a lean build, and an unmistakable mole on his right cheek. A small curly-haired Greek sat to his right, and a large blond bearded Dutchman to his left.

"I wish that bloody bastard would break his neck," said James Bradley under his breath in a smarmy, affected British accent that he always used to his advantage.

As soon as the train was out of sight, Bradley, Hansie, and Max descended the stairs of the hotel and crossed the road. Entering his office a few minutes later, they were greeted by Bradley's secretary Beatrice, a plucky young woman with coiffed short hair and an uneasy red lip-sticked smile. Bradley shoved his hat into her waiting hands, and the others did the same. As she moved to hang them up, he slapped her playfully on the derriere, causing her to turn and look at them with an admonishment and flushed pink cheeks. Hansie laughed, revealing his tobacco-stained teeth, as Beatrice hurried embarrassedly back to her desk without a word. The whole interaction made Max uncomfortable.

Once Bradley was seated behind his oversized mahogany desk, Max and Hansie flopped down opposite him in the leather armchairs.

"You know it is still beyond me. Why do you want that land of his so badly, Mr. Bradley? Farming is not your cup of tea, as you say."

"That is none of your bloody business Max? Stay out of it, you hear me? Just remember how easily you could be the subject of a random hunting accident. You know they happen all the time in Africa." he smiled slyly at Hansie.

"And besides, you fool, I don't want Demberra for the land," said Bradley with indignation. "Something that belongs to me is buried there. Something Sutton stole from that old kaffir Mamba in Barotseland that's rightfully mine. That's why we will be paying the old man a little visit soon for some retribution. Sutton's kaffir is the old man's son, so Sutton's keeping up the ruse, see?" Again, he and Hansie shared a look of understanding between them.

Max persisted, his dark eyes deep with curiosity. "Can't you just take what is yours. Sneak up there when he's away?"

"Because Sutton built a fucking verandah over it, didn't he?

"He must have some secret access to it from inside the house," added Hansie to beef up the story. Max's eyes grew wide. He wasn't the brightest bulb.

"When that kaffir reported his gold missing, fucking Sutton blamed it on me, and I had the coppers up my arse for the next three months. So, why do you think I got a hold of Mattias King's land a few months ago after his unfortunate demise? It's a bargaining chip, that's all. And that's why you're both here. Demberra has to be mine legally, so I can claim what's rightfully mine." Bradley said, leaning back in his chair.

"Now get out of here, Max, and go and get me a bottle of scotch. I have some business here with Hansie."

As soon as the door to Bradley's office shut, Hansie laughed loudly. Beatrice shuffled some papers on her desk, reminding them she was still there.

"You too, darlin. Go and fix your makeup or something. Scram!" Beatrice didn't need to be told twice and scurried out the front door without her hat and gloves.

"That little shit has no idea." sneered Hansie. "Just like Jaun and that kid."

"Absolutely not. Let's keep it that way. Max and that Afrikaner are ticking time bombs, but we will still need Max, he'll be useful later. But he has a big mouth, and I don't trust him, so just keep letting him believe Sutton stole it. As for this kid Siddley, he's an anomaly. Seems like a straight-up prep school kid, but he has some sort of vendetta against Sutton for some reason, he won't tell me why. Either way, we can use him until he isn't useful anymore. Free labor."

"That was some brilliant storytelling, sir. When did we steal that gold from the kaffir? "I remember that night, creeping out of there in the dark. Had to be at least eight years ago. Good thing those kaffirs couldn't nail you," said Hansie.

"People in high places, Hansie." He winked. "It was right after Van Wyk got sick and left. Long before Max moved here," Bradley continued. "Who knew this fucking Mick would show up out of the blue and lay claim to the land? And he's so bloody hard to get rid of. But my friend, the price of gold has been rising on the black market, especially since the Depression, so maybe we should be thanking Mr. Sutton for the delay. We could be looking at a whopping thirteen thousand pounds."

"That's some serious money," said Hansie rubbing his hands together greedily. "So, what do you have planned for Sutton and his girl? I'll say Sutton is one lucky bastard to have snatched up not only that land but also that fine young girl. He acts like he's her guardian, but he's had plenty of nights alone with her in that big house where no one can hear them." Hansie said, grinning lasciviously with is awful teeth.

"I've made sure the locals are aware of his escapades, and they all agree. He's a dirty fucking pig!" Bradley laughed

"But no one speaks up because he is chummy with that fat inspector. I'm tired of it. That bastard has reaped far too many benefits. But all that is about to change. He will soon have two choices: He can go and set up his pathetic excuse of a farm elsewhere with his little whore, or he can hand it over and make me an offer to look after her once he's bankrupt. Then I'll show her what a real man is all about."

Hansie leaned back in his chair and laughed. "Sir, you are going to ruin him." he laughed viciously.

"Well, I better get going, sir. Someone has to keep an eye on that little Greek." Hansie shook Bradley's hand and bumped into Beatrice on his way out, giving her an uncomfortable once-over.

Bradley swiveled in his chair to face Beatrice, who was trying to ignore his burning stare. He blew her a salacious kiss as she caught his eye. His slimy laugh made her wriggle back in her seat. Gratefully he swiveled his chair back to face the window as he stared out across town to the tracks. His mind began to wander to the pretty teenage girl he had last seen board the train to Bulawayo with Tom. The vantage point from his office window was enlightening.

A hungry grin spread across Bradley's face, and his trousers became a little tighter as he imagined himself indulging in more than just monetary rewards. It wasn't fair that Sutton had her all to himself. How fulfilling it would be to take his land and his ravishing young ward with it, to do with as he pleased. He turned his chair back around to face Beatrice and began to unbutton his trousers.

CHAPTER 7

WEASEL BYRNE THE ZAMBEZI TRADER

Barotseland, home of the Lozi people, had once been a vast area, as large as the German Empire, that stretched across the upper Zambezi floodplain. Barotseland saw its pinnacle during the reign of Lewanika, the conqueror, in the late 1800s. Preceded by a century of bloodshed and consolidation of tribes through usurped power and subjugation, the Lozi had amassed a sizable kingdom developed largely through asn indisputable dependence on slave labor. Lewanika's defeat of the Matabele tribe had earned him the respect of his people, and like most tribes in the region, the Lozi believed that the spoils of war belonged to the victor. Their expansive land offered fertile soil for crops and pasture for their short-horn cattle. Fish, maize, cattle, milk, ivory, and often slaves were traded with the Portuguese in exchange for European goods and weapons.

As colonization spread across the continent and tribes continued to war for territory, Lewanika became anxious to retain control of Barotseland and naturally saw the benefits of an alliance with the British South African Company. So, with the help of French Missionaries, the king entered into an agreement with the British, and in 1890 Barotseland became a protected nation-state under the

British South African Company in exchange for mineral rights on his land. Lewanika believed that with their protection, he could preserve his authority, protect his people, and save the Lozi hierarchy.

Lewanika helped expand the Ngonye Canal, connecting much of the Zambezi and expanding trade routes. His friendship and hospitality to French Missionaries helped bring modern education to his people. However, Lewanika soon became disillusioned with his agreement with the British South African Company (BSAC), and despite gifts of placation and a trip to London for the coronation of Edward VII as a guest of the Crown, they failed to pay the agreed-upon annual stipend, a condition of the agreement. White settlers soon arrived in the East, and Lewanika's kingdom was severed in half in the Anglo-Portuguese Agreement. His power within the colony had been officially restricted.

In 1906 the British Crown demanded that Lewanika abolish slavery in Barotseland, a system that had profited the Lozi and one that Lewanika relied on for Barotseland's wealth and prosperity. Dutifully he issued an emancipation proclamation, but it only went so far as the ink it was written with, and Barotseland and its Lozi elite continued to operate on the infrastructure of serfdom while the BSAC conveniently turned a blind eye and collected its taxes.

Lewanika died in 1916, the same year as the Easter Rising in Ireland, and his son Litia, or Yeta as he was better known to the British, was now the new king of Barotseland. Litia, like his father, also recognized that the Lozi hierarchy would break if they abolished tribute labor, and he had picked up his father's mantle arguing against the abolition of slavery. But opinions against slavery had become more acute, and this time the British demanded full abolition. After much deliberation, Litia begrudgingly accepted an annual payment as compensation, and in 1925, he officially ended slavery and indentured servitude in Barotseland.

Considering his dealings with the British, Litia and his headmen had become wary of agreements with any white man. Simalala's father, Mambo, had fought the Matebele bravely alongside Chief Lewanika and, like the Chief and later his son Litia, was also wary of white men. But though his son Simalala, Mambo had learned of Tom's own checkered past with the British, and they shared mutual feelings of distrust and injustice. So, it was for these reasons and Simalala's personal connection that his father, Mambo, had agreed to sell cattle to Tom and no other white men in the region.

Simalala, who was usually not a man of many words, always became an animated storyteller on their journeys to his homeland, elaborating on tales of his father's bravery and prowess in the defeat of the Matabele. Tom had heard the story about how the Matabele had tried to escape the great Zambezi downstream in stolen Macoras[7] at least three times before. Not dissimilar in emotion from the war stories, he and Weasel often shared about their time in the IRA.

According to Simalala, bad luck or poor navigation had led the outnumbered Matabele warriors to their demise when they landed on an island in the middle of the Zambezi, believing it to be the river's shore. Simalala's father had led the attack to retrieve the stolen Macoras,[7] leaving them stranded on the island as the river flooded. Once the Barotse had trapped the enemy, they systematically executed them or starved them to death, explained Simalala with pride and bravado.

The violence of war and insurrection had become a welcomed distant memory for Tom, and it felt discordant reconciling Simalala's gentle and congenial nature with that kind of barbarism. Centuries of warring African tribes and alternating massacres were challenging to follow for the most adept historian. But regardless of who was right or wrong in the scheme of things, he couldn't deny that he had little right to judge their violent history, considering the atrocities Europeans had perpetrated on each other for centuries, including the ones he had seen first-hand in the twentieth century.

So, he listened politely as Simalala carried on about the great war with the Matabele, expounding on the Barotse people's right as victors to leave their enemy to drown mercilessly or be dragged off half-dead by crocodiles to rot in their lairs before consumption.

---

[7]   A boat made from a hollowed-out tree trunk

Tom liked to think humanity could be better than this. Did all warring tribes have to resort to these measures of murder, rape, and violence? Couldn't human beings just be peaceful and etch out a life for themselves in some semi-noble way without fear of invasion, suppression, or enslavement. He realized he was a different man than he had been ten years ago when the pursuit of freedom from what he deemed to be oppression had ruled his heart and mind. He had been an idealist. But as his mind wandered from Simalala's images of savagery to his own indiscretions, he wondered if his own sacrifice had been worth it. Had his personal losses been worth the fight for freedom? A freedom that he now couldn't and wouldn't partake in? He could still be breathing the crisp Irish country air in the arms of his adoring wife and son if it hadn't been for men's lust for power and wealth.

As they crossed the river on the barge, Tom thought of the lake back home and the serenity he had always felt near the water. He looked at Simalala, who was now humming a song in Lozi, staring serenely ahead as the barge moved methodically through the water. Tom reflected on how much his life had changed. He could never have fathomed at twenty-five that fifteen years later, he would be standing on a barge with a black man in the middle of Africa, journeying willingly into the bush to meet a tribal leader to buy cattle for his ranch. And with these cattle, he would grow and expand his farm for a girl, who had become his daughter and was the only creature worth living for.

He had to smile at the turn of events. Maybe this was redemption, he thought, as he allowed his eyes to fill, comforted that he could feel the weight of these emotions in daylight, out here on this great river where no one could witness his pain, his gratefulness, or his longing as he stared out over the water.

After the barge was tied down, Tom and Simalala pushed the lorry, called a truck, after all, it was American onto dry land and climbed in. Leaving the serenity of the river behind, they began down the narrow road that they had carved together with some of Simalala's men the first time they had traveled here four years ago. It made Tom breathe a little easier, knowing that only he and Simalala knew of this route. Tom was confident that Len would have arrived by way of Sesheke and then journey upriver from there by boat. It would be at least two more days before they reached Weasel. Tom's Ford truck had been a worthwhile purchase, not just for the farm but for ventures into the bush just like this.

The grasses were high on either side, and the ground was uneven as the truck rattled along the makeshift road. They had been wise enough to dig trenches on both sides of the rude roadway to handle runoff if they might need to use it during the rainy season. Tom was thankful that this was not the case today.

Over the years, he had come to feel quite at home in this wild land but couldn't deny that it was comforting to have Simalala's company. Simalala knew the bush like no white man, and that was never to be disregarded. As they moved deeper northward, the dense bush eventually cleared to a plain where sable, impala, kudu, and herds of buffaloes roamed freely. With the rainy season behind them, the game was out in full throng. Although they were well hidden, Tom was distinctly aware of native surveillance as they moved into Lozi territory and was again grateful for Simalala's companionship. As the afternoon sun blazed through the window and the truck continued over uneven terrain, Tom tipped his hat over his eyes and leaned back to capture a few minutes of rest, grateful that he had taken the time to teach his companion how to drive.

Over the next two days, the two men took turns driving, sleeping at night in the truck. By sunset on the second night, they had traversed a mere ninety miles, although the obstacle-ridden journey seemed more like nine hundred miles to Tom. By nightfall, they entered the outpost. The small, disheveled town had grown up since they were last here. More thatched houses than he remembered had cropped up near Weasel's place. Even the small beer hall nearby looked like it had been updated. A two-room police station and mission building with an adjoining chapel now rounded out the little village. Tom pulled his truck up in front of the familiar red brick storefront. A new white sign outside read "Trading Post and Residence of T. Byrne."

"You think he's here, Bwana?" said Simalala as they pulled in. "For his sake, I hope so!" said Tom. But before he could turn off the ignition, a hand reached in through his open window and pushed a gun into the nape of his neck and growled some muffled orders in a thick Afrikaans accent.

"Turn off the engine and get out. Tell him to do the same and come out poly poly[8]. Don't try to outsmart the Greener." he snarled, pushing the gun aggressively into Tom's neck, as a large accomplice appeared at Simalala's door raising a similar gun to his face.

"Where's your boss?" said Tom feeling the blood rise to his face. He didn't know these men and wondered what this greeting was all about.

"Turn off the engine and get out," the man repeated. As Tom turned the key in the ignition to oblige, his mind drifted to the Dutchman's revolver laying on the seat between them. But the guard was quick and whacked Tom hard with the side of the gun.

"I can see it, min. Get out!" said the man smugly with a thick Afrikaans accent. Realizing they had no retaliation, Tom nodded to Simalala, and they exited the truck as his captor grabbed his left arm and spat with disgust on the ground beside him. With his free hand, Tom rubbed the rising bump on his head and walked in step next to Simalala, who had the barrel of a gun affixed to the back of his head.

It at been two years since Tom had been to Weasel's establishment. In addition to the henchmen, a lot had changed since they were last at the trading post. The whole store had been renovated by the looks of it, saving no expense. They passed through the shop, which seemed larger and far more organized than it had been before. Bins of dried goods, coffee, and tobacco were stacked against one wall. Four neat shelves ran the length of the other, displaying everything from milled soaps and fabrics to medicines and spices. Crockery and dishes graced the front window, along with some carefully chosen handcrafted furniture and fancy imported table lamps. In the corner, several various shiny new farming implements and machinery

---

[8]   slowly

sat tagged with their asking prices. He even had a cash register now and an assortment of confections and licorice in jars on the counter.

It was a real general store, and despite Tom's aching head, he was impressed. Beyond the store, the men led them down a thirty-foot passageway with what appeared to be storerooms on either side. This must lead to his new living quarters, Tom surmised. As they approached the closed door, he could hear voices and see a faint light spilling from beneath the door.

The harsh light momentarily blinded them as the door swung open. Against the wall, sprawled out on a large couch, lounged Weasel with a glass of whisky in one hand and a pistol in the other. It took a second for Tom to register the image before him. Weasel's hair was cut short and slicked back in a modern style. He had gained a few pounds, which looked well on him. He wore a maroon jacquard robe and loose trousers and looked entirely comfortable in his surroundings.

The sizable room was quite exquisite, with rich dark furniture, a brightly colored Oriental rug adorning the rough concrete floor underneath, and several brass lamps. Fine paintings graced the walls, and a crystal decanter and glasses sat poised on the mahogany end table next to Weasel.

Sitting in the chair opposite Weasel's couch, and slanted in his direction, was a young woman. Tom was instantly captivated and simultaneously damaged by her stare. Her black hair was unfashionably long and fell wild and loose over her shoulders. The thin ivory kaftan robe she wore floated gently against her milk chocolate skin like sheets wavering on a clothesline. Her feet were bare, but her toes were painted a bright red. Her far-away bronze eyes encroached on his personal space.

"Be Jaysus, Jesus, Mary, and holy Saint Joseph. If it isn't the one and only Thomas Sutton." bellowed Weasel, almost losing the grasp on his glass and jumping to greet Tom.

"What have you done to yourself? You look like a bloody Arabian Prince." laughed Tom as Weasel rushed over, embracing him with gusto.

"And you brought Simalala along? How are you, you big Muntu?" laughed Weasel shaking Simalala's hand vigorously, to the dismay of his henchmen.

"I am good, Bwana Weasel. How are you?"

"I am well, too. Bloody hell, I am so happy to see you two here after such a long time. "I gather you have met my bodyguards," said Weasel apologizing as he gestured to their escorts.

"Indeed, we have, but we have not been formally introduced," said Tom rubbing the bump on his head again unconsciously.

Upset that they'd been treated roughly, Weasel laughed awkwardly and attempted to lighten the mood by embellishing his guards' backstories. The man who stood behind Simalala was a German named Friedrich Holtz, whose name Weasel butchered mercilessly with his Irish tongue. Apparently, he had spent some time in the twenties in Southwest Africa. Undoubtedly a hooligan, Tom thought. The German squinted at the introduction.

Tom's guard was introduced as Mooi Boetie, and a flame of familiarity flickered in Tom's mind. Now in the light, he recalled that he'd seen the man once, at a distant, some years before and had heard plenty about him from Weasel. His reputation matched his sculking figure, square jawline, and thick black eyebrows.

"Ah, so you're that pretty boy from the mines of the Rand?
Weasel has told me a lot about you."

"I had no idea you were a friend of Timmy's." scoffed the man.

"Look, mate, maybe be more mindful on your next encounter with visitors. Doesn't matter who they are. That kind of greeting is a bad image for the business." Tom said and punctuated his statement with a sharp blow to Boetie's temple.

"And that's for the bloody bump on my head."

And then he curled his knuckles white again and added a swift punch to the man's gut, proclaiming, "that's for Simalala."

The second attack took the wind out of Mooi Bootie, and he stumbled backward, falling into the wall behind him. Weasel only smirked. The German, not wanting a similar fate, stood motionless as Simalala glared at him menacingly.

"You still have that killer streak in you, Tom. You don't mess with Tom Sutton, boys. You'll remember that next time, right? Leave us now." Weasel concluded with a stare of authority as Mooi Bootie stumbled back to his feet.

Still clutching his gut and scowling, he picked up his hat and dusted off his knees, gestured to the German, and they swiftly left the room. Tom threw Simalala the truck keys, and, taking the signal, he excused himself so the old friends could talk. The woman remained in the room, watching the whole scenario unfold without averting her eyes once.

In the absence of his guards, Weasel instantly became the animated host. Grabbing the bottle of whiskey beside him, he gave Tom a hefty pour and refilled his own, and gestured to the empty chair across from the woman. Tom sat, trying not to stare at her.

She spoke to Weasel while keeping her eyes fixed on Tom. "Who is this, Señor Timothy? she inquired in a thick Portuguese accent.

"This man, Maria, is my old friend, Thomas Sutton, from the Mother Country. And please girlie, stop calling me Senor, will you? It's just Weasel or Tim or Timothy if you must! He said irritably. Clearly, this wasn't the first time.

"It's a pleasure to meet you, Maria," said Tom attempting to sound nonchalant while quickly averting his eyes back to Weasel.

"What the bloody hell are you up to, Weasel, excuse my French lass? said Tom jovially. It was good to see Weasel again. He made him feel connected to the best part of his past, and he couldn't deny how much he had missed that.

"Señor, you are a fighter, no?" asked Maria, again staring directly at Tom.

"Tom and I fought together for Ireland. In hand-to-hand combat. So yes, I'd say Tom was pretty unbeatable." smiled Weasel as he gulped a mouthful of liquor.

"Weasel is too flattering…and I'm sorry that you had to see that, Maria," said Tom earnestly, turning to look at her. Embarrassed, he took her hand gently and kissed the back in apology. He rarely had the occasion to be in the presence of females other than the wives of his African farm workers, local Livingstone dames, and Heidi, with whom he never had to put on any show. But Maria disarmed him and made him feel nervous. He hadn't felt this way for a long time.

"Well, Señor Tom, I would trust you to defend me if I found myself on the wrong side," whispered Maria softly as she retreated her hand and rose from her seat. "I am tired, Timothy. I'll leave you two old friends to converse, to talk." she clarified and floated out of the room, presumably to her bedroom, only dropping Tom's gaze when she disappeared from the door frame.

Tom stared at Weasel for a few moments before speaking. "So… fill me in," said Tom enthusiastically with a grin.

"About business or the girl?" said Weasel pouring himself another glass,

"Well, how long have you known her?"

"A few months. I traded with her father, a Portuguese fellow. I got to know him well…nice man. Her mother died of the Spanish Flu in 1919 when she was no more than Heidi's age, and she was very close to her father. So, she pretty much grew up alongside him as a trader, never married. She had no other family. They lived in Mozambique, where all the Portuguese are firmly established. Anyway, I was supposed to meet with him in Beira, and it turns out he died of malaria before Christmas. I found her there alone, and she begged me to take her with me. There wasn't anything left there for her, least of all money. Her father had some bad debts, and I suppose the bloody Irish Catholic guilt got the best of me."

"So? are you two…?" asked Tom with a wink.

Weasel laughed. "I'd be lying if I said I hadn't hoped something might come of it, Thomas. The nights can get cold out here all alone, if you know what I mean. But I brought her here under the condition that she help me at the post, no strings attached. She has a keen business sense, and she understands how to operate in a man's world. She's also smart enough to know what life for an unmarried woman would be like alone. So, she helps me with the business and adds a feminine touch around here and there, as you can see, and I make sure no harm comes to her. Very unsatisfactorily platonic." said Weasel.

Tom sighed with more gratitude than he had wanted to, and they clinked glasses.

"Enough of Maria. What brings you all the way out here, Tom?"

"Well, I wish it was just a social visit, Weasel," said Tom pulling his chair closer.

Weasel's face turned grim. "Be out with it, Tom."

"You might be getting an unexpected visit from Len Johnston soon enough. Gold smuggling? He's onto you. If he's headed all the way here, he must have gathered some proof that's not in your favor."

"Who in the bloody hell told you that, Sutton?" Weasel asked, combing his brain for a snitch.

"Let's just say, the last time I met Len, he shared this with me. I suppose he was hoping I'd do just this…inform you so you'd have time to fix things. Based on your face, I presume he has enough to charge you with?"

Weasel didn't waste a moment and shot up off the couch. Heading to his desk in the far corner, he pressed a button on the wall, and within seconds, Mooi Boetie and Holtz barged through the door behind Tom. For a moment, Tom caught the glint of hate in men's eyes as they pushed past him and stood before Weasel, awaiting instructions.

Maybe Weasel hadn't anticipated this. But years of covert operations under the employ of the Irish Republic had served him well in this operation. His accommodation was conveniently located in the town of Katimo Mulilo along the Northern Rhodesian side of the Zambezi. The rest of the establishments were idle and inconspicuously spread alongside the river in Southwest Africa, where little controlled navigational transport existed, and the west bank was yet to be discovered by colonists. His strategy was well envisioned and had given Weasel a commanding power over his operation, the men he employed, and the wealth he had accumulated. An excess of seven thousand pounds, all in gold, he had divulged to Tom.

"Get everything out and put it in spot number four. Not a trace or a single strand of hair can be left behind if we get a surprise visit by the law in the next few days."

Weasel projected an air of calm and strategy, but inside he felt the blood rushing to his brain. Who could have tipped Len off? Who could he trust now? He didn't have time to second-guess things. He had to move his stash and fast. He looked at Tom. His presence was like a stabilizing rod, and he was grateful for it.

Watching Weasel pour over maps and plans with these men made Tom uneasy. It wasn't his place to judge his friend's operations, he told himself. He was gratefully ignorant of the details and intended to keep it that way for both their sakes. He had worked too hard above board for years to be pulled into this now, regardless of how much money it was. He was here to support his old friend and nothing more.

Boetie and Holtz have now gone to load up their bush truck. Weasel pulled his hands through his already slick hair and sighed loudly. Tom stood and approached his desk.

"Do you trust your so-called guards?"

"Well, let's say I'll be watching them move it tonight, and I'll go behind them tomorrow and move it again. It's not only them I worry about. Anyone could be after it if it got to Len's ears in Livingstone."

Tom was glad that his friend was shrewd and nodded in understanding. Weasel had started as Mooi Boetie's partner years ago, and Tom wondered if he'd turn on Weasel given half the chance. He'd known his type before: loyalty was bought and paid for.

"I figure I have at least a day, maybe two, until the coppers arrive. You're the only one I trust, you know?" Weasel said, looking visibly worried.

"I know," said Tom earnestly. "But tell me no more. It's better for both of us this way. Just be careful. You have no more than two days at best. I'd handle it tonight if I were you. I'll hold down the fort here until you get back, just in case he arrives."

A few minutes later, Weasel emerged in khaki trousers and heavy boots. He offered Tom his bedroom and suggested Simalala take the couch, although he knew the African would rather probably stay outside in the truck keeping watch.

"Right then! I'll be back tomorrow morning if all goes well. Take care of Maria and keep an eye out for anything suspicious. If the law comes here, either make yourself scarce or have a good story, boyo. It won't look good for you if I'm not back."

Tom agreed, and Weasel left, slamming the door behind him. He was grateful Weasel hadn't asked him to come. He pulled off the dirty boots he'd worn for the last fifty hours and discarded them, rubbing his moist feet one by one. There was a knock at the door. It was Simalala. Seeing Weasel and the men leave in a flurry had alarmed him, and he came to bring Tom the revolver.

"You can sleep in here if you want." offered Tom explaining what had transpired.

"No, Bwana, I sleep in the truck. I can watch better that way." "Then you keep this then," Tom said, handing back the revolver. He nodded in understanding and left. As soon as the door closed behind him, Tom locked it and, grabbing his boots, retreated to Weasel's bedroom in the hope of catching a few hours of rest.

He was grateful that Weasel had had the good sense to install a modern bathroom, despite his disdain for baths. Frustrated and sweaty, he pulled off his road-weary clothes and ran through the water. A hot bath and good night's sleep before all hell broke loose on Weasel's scheme was just what he needed. Laying in the bathtub, he stared out the window. The sky was bright outside. It was a full moon, and the night sky was well-lit. This was good for Weasel, thought Tom. It would make his task easier. But how far out was Len? And did Len really have concrete proof? And how was he going to stay out of this mess?

His mind wandered from Weasel to Heidi and back again until the water turned cold, and his fingers became noticeably wrinkled. Climbing out of the tub, he dried quickly, wrapping a fresh towel around his waist, cursing the fact that he'd left his change of clothes in the truck. He pulled a cigar from the breast pocket of his discarded shirt and moved back into the bedroom, and sat on the edge of the bed. Well, at least he was clean, he thought, and the bed looked warm and inviting.

The double bed, with its polished brass posts, was fancier than he had expected from Weasel. But Weasel had never had anything rich in his life. He deserved it, didn't he? He lit the cigar, laid back, and allowed his mind to wander. Jealousy invaded his thoughts this time. Here was his friend living a comfortable, uncomplicated life. Where had all his honesty and hard work got him anyway? Demberra was successful now, but what if he lost it? Maybe he should have gotten involved with Weasel years ago. Then Heidi's bright eyes laced with admiration and respect for him brought him back. She was his future, his responsibility. And what was the price of Weasel's success? He knew that he would never have to live in fear of the law, mistrust his employees or covet a woman who didn't love him.

Poor Weasel, Tom thought. He was a good man at the core and a true friend. He had pulled him back from the brink once, and he vowed he would be here for him in his time of need as much as he was able. As Tom inhaled the last puff of his cigar, he heard the door creak gently open. He felt vulnerable, lying naked under the bedclothes, without a weapon. He quickly slid to the edge of the bed and wrapped the top quilt around him. He tamped out the cigar and grabbed a knife that lay on Weasel's nightstand. Old habits don't die easily, he thought as he grasped the handle and approached the door.

"Don't take another step, or you're a dead man."

A soft voice responded. "Or a dead woman, Señor?" said Maria pushing the door open.

He quickly realized his compromising position and wrapped the quilt tighter around his waist, his naked chest on full display.

Apart from a few unsavory and unmemorable trysts during his nights of drunken debauchery in Cape Town, Tom had remained in a self-imposed state of penitential celibacy since he had adopted Heidi. The midnight moonlight that now streamed through the window behind him illuminated the outline of Maria's face and her long black hair as it tumbled over her shoulders. He couldn't take his eyes off the curves of her body as her white silk nightgown caressed her frame in all the right places. She moved closer, and he could hear her breathing.

How did you know I was in here? He said, stumbling over his words and retreating to the bed as she advanced, sitting on the bottom of it.

"I saw Señor Tim leave," she said gently but affirmatively.

"Do you mind if I sit Señor Tom?" she asked but didn't wait for a response. Maria approached the bed and sat on the edge, placing some distance between them. She pulled her knees up underneath her, stretching her nightgown over them.

"Is something bothering you, Maria?"

"I am sorry. I was curious, Señor Tom. How do you know Señor Tim?"

"Tom … please call me Tom. We have been friends for a long time, Weasel, I mean Tim and me. We grew up in Ireland together. We've seen good times and bad ones too. And what about you and him? How long have you known each other?"

"Señor Tim brought me here to Barotseland from Beira. When my father died, I had nowhere to turn as an unmarried woman with no formal education. But I know the business of trading. And I can cook and keep house, so I convinced him to take me along to help him. But on nights like these, I miss my father and my home. But there's nothing left for me there anymore."

Maria looked so fragile and vulnerable at that moment, like a child. He couldn't begin to understand what trials she may have faced getting here, and he suspected that she rarely let her guard down like this. It couldn't be easy, surrounded by all these misfits. Weasel didn't mistreat her. Tom was sure of that. But his friend could be dismissive and insensitive, especially to women. Over the years, he had hardened, mostly for self-preservation, Tom guessed.

Tom, on the other hand, had become quite skilled in tenderness. Raising a teenage daughter as a single man had taught him nuance and sensitivity. He didn't always understand women, but he was perceptive to their emotions and responsive to the obstacles they faced, even in the twentieth century. She couldn't be more than twenty-six or twenty-seven, he thought as he reached for her hand and turned to face her as she remained curled up on the edge of the bed. She accepted his kindness.

"If you aren't happy here, can't you go home?" "You must have some family in Beira?"

"No, I don't," said Maria choking on her words a little.

"It's money that keeps me here, Senor Tom. You see, if I stay here with Señor …I mean Tim. Someday I'll have enough to go back to Beira and buy my own house and maybe set up a little store. My father worked with Tim many times and trusted him. I do too. But it's not time yet." she said resolutely. "But that doesn't change how lonely I feel sometimes."

Tom could feel her hand shivering in his, and at that moment, all he wanted to do was protect her from the damage.

"Are you cold, Maria." "Yes, Señor Tom."

"It's just Tom, Maria."

"Sorry…Thomas. I didn't think of bringing my shawl when I came here. I don't even know why I came. It's only that I recognized the pain in your eyes. The same look my father had his whole life after my mother died and the same look that I see in my own eyes sometimes."

Tom moved closer to her and pulled a loose blanket off the bed, and wrapped it around both their shoulders while keeping his lower half covered with the quilt. Maria moved closer to him and rested her face against his chest. He didn't care anymore that he was half naked. He pulled her into him and wrapped the blanket tightly around them.

Am I right?" Maria continued.

"Yes," said Tom after a few moments of silence. His guarded heart was in fear of being breached. He had never spoken deeply about his losses with anyone other than Weasel. Yet somehow, he knew she would understand. He leaned back on the bed, releasing the blanket. But she followed, unraveling the blanket and placing it gently over them both. She pulled herself close to him and laid her head on his chest, where she could hear his heart beating faster. She said nothing but grasped his hand in hers with a tenderness he hadn't felt since…he didn't want to go back there now, back to the cottage, back to Grace and Sean. But it was too late, and he couldn't stop the tears from escaping.

She lifted herself on one elbow and looked deeply into his eyes. "How long ago did you lose her…your love?" she said gently without judgment.

"My loves," he said in barely a whisper. "Ten years, seven months, and twelve days"

"Loves?" she questioned

"My wife and my little son too… and it was all my fault." "Sometimes, doesn't your heart feel like it will break. And you wonder if living is worth it all." Maria said, wiping the tears from his cheek. "Then you remember that they would want you to live. We live for them because they can't live for us."

She leaned down and kissed him gently on the lips. Her touch felt like a balm for his wounded heart. He stroked her long hair and closed his eyes, pulling her to him. Their lips met again, pressing deeper. Tongues entangled, searching for connection. He moved to her neck. She smelled like summer flowers. She was alive and warm and broken, just like him. Maria fell to his side, letting her hair fall around her. He was now over her and took a moment to soak her in, tracing a line with one finger down the side of her face, to her throat, between her breasts, and to her waist. This was visceral. He was wholly present. He could see her breathe. She was alive, and he was alive.

She pulled him to her and kissed him again deeply. His hands found the buttons on her gown and began to unbutton them. He pealed the soft material back to admire her.

The moonlight that filtered through the curtained window caressed her naked body, and she smiled up at him with her whole face. He traced his finger around each breast as her nipples responded to his touch. He sucked on one, then the other, and Maria let out a soft groan. She allowed his hand to travel underneath her nightgown and between her legs. She was naked underneath, and she could feel him harden and throb against her. He stroked the inside of her thighs, moving closer to her treasure, and she moved against him rhythmically. She wanted him. He gently pushed aside her nightgown and slowly eased himself into her. He found her mouth again, and they locked together, building a pace in unison, punctuated by groans of pleasure. He didn't want to be anywhere but right here in her arms. As the moon faded from view and the early morning became dark, they finally drifted into sleep, tangled together in a mess of blankets and abandoned clothing.

At the first sign of sunlight, Maria opened her eyes, her eyelashes brushing Tom's chest. For a moment, she felt no regret. He had needed her as much as she had needed him in this world of broken promises. For the first time in her adult life, she felt alive, and she had chosen this for herself; She had chosen him.

She deftly extricated herself from the bedclothes, pulling her gown back on silently as Tom slept. Tears began to heave from her chest, and she knew she had to get out because she couldn't control them. At the bedroom door, she looked back at him through her tears.

"Take care of yourself, my Señor Tom, for I shared my only treasure with you this night."

CHAPTER 8

THE SNITCH

Tom awoke to laughter. He disentangled himself from a web of sheets and blankets and stumbled naked to the bathroom, where he relieved himself and moved to the small ceramic sink next to the toilet and splashed cold water on his face. He stared at himself in the mirror. His eyes were alert, and his hair was slightly more than normally disheveled, but his face seemed oddly unrecognizable. Then every moment of the night before collided simultaneously in his mind as his ears perked to the noises outside.

"Oh, God! What had he done? Where was Maria? Who was here? Weasel was going to kill him. And where the hell were his clothes, God damn it!" His mind raced.

"Simalala," he called in a whispered scream from the bedroom window.

He could see the truck from here. In the light of day, he now stood at the edge of the bed and witnessed where he and Maria had spent their night. His eyes widened in shock, and he quickly pulled up the sheets and blankets as the laughter and conversation from the other room grew louder.

Simalala knocked loudly at the window. His eyes danced with amusement at the sight of Tom's nakedness and agitation.

"Bwana Tom, you shout like a woman in a child. And I cannot remember leaving you like a Barotse warrior last night."

"Alright, alright," said Tom irritably. "It's not funny. Where the hell are my bloody clothes, Simalala? I have been robbed."

Simalala shook his head, chuckling at his misfortune, and retreated to the truck returning with a leather knapsack. He laughed as he passed Tom the bag through the window, earning him a second glare.

As Tom began to rummage through the bag, he could hear Simalala roaring in laughter as he made his way back to the truck. He managed to pull on a clean pair of rumpled undershorts from his travel bag, catching himself as he tripped one-legged and nearly hit the bed frame. The door opened. His eyes met Maria's deep stare.

"Do you intend to sabotage my life, Señor Tom?"

"What?" he said, taken off guard. His eyes surveyed her body as he relived their night together. She wore an unpretentious white cotton sundress tied at the waist with a navy-blue scarf. Her hair hung in a long braid down her back. She was more radiant than last night, more beautiful but distant.

She shifted nervously under his gaze and then broke the connection by crossing to the bed and laying down his freshly washed and pressed clothing. She turned to face him and cleared her throat to interrupt the unnerving silence.

"I thought you would want fresh clothes, Señor Tom," she said matter-of-factly, avoiding eye contact.

"Please, it's just Tom or Thomas. Thank You, Maria," he said flatly. She nodded and started to remove the bedding.

"Wait! "Why? Why me?" Tom said softly. She looked up, returning his gaze with inscrutable eyes. They stayed locked, searching for each other's intentions.

"Because you're different. You are not like any other man I have encountered here or in Beira. You have a deep pain that I understand, and you are lost like me." Maria said deliberately.

But you… you were a virgin. Weasel made me think otherwise. And …you barely know me." Tom said, trying to understand the gravity of her gift.

Maria wasn't insulted by Tom's query. A chaste unattached woman living amongst male traders was certainly unusual. Fortunately for her, her father had been a modern thinker, and after her mother died, they shared a bond of mutual respect. He trusted that she would make a good match for herself when the time was right. So, Maria had managed to escape marriage proposals and vile propositions since she had come of age, under the protection of her father. If Weasel had known her father, he must have known this. This must be why he had offered her safety, domicile, and employment for as long as she needed it, even if it hurt his ego. It had been a fair arrangement for Maria given the circumstances, that was until she met Tom.

"No, I am not a whore, Thomas. When my father died, I couldn't stay in Beira alone, you understand. Your friend, Tim, is a very generous man. He took me in. He pays me to take care of the house, and I help him with his work. And in return, I have a place to live, and I can save a little money for my future, as I told you. Many have tried to steal me away, some roughly and some with sweet, flowery lies. But you are not like these men. You have strong convictions. You are kind, and while you are strong on the outside, you are fragile within. I gave myself to you of my own will. I wanted to know you, Thomas…to understand you."

Tom was dumbfounded. She was obviously waiting for some validation that her confession hadn't been for naught. But he just stared at her, lost for words. She dropped her gaze and continued to remove the soiled sheets and blankets without a word as he watched her. She gathered up the bundle and made for her exit.

"Maria, if I had known that you… then I never would have touched you." He stammered, blurting out the first thing that came to his lips, immediately regretting his pronouncement.

She stopped at the door and turned to face him, her eyes wounded and misty.

"You brought light into my life, don't you understand. I thought I gave you the same. I thought you could be someone I could love."

She hastily wiped her eyes with the edge of the sheets, straightened her posture, and silently slid out of the room, leaving Tom staring at the void she left in her wake. His mind swirled with visions of Maria and Grace. His heart pulsed between excitement and fear as adrenaline vibrated through his body. He couldn't make sense of what he was feeling and suddenly again became acutely aware of the voices outside the door.

He forced himself from his trance and grabbed the pile of neatly folded clothes Maria had left him, returning his change of clothes to his knapsack. He could at least accept her kind gesture, couldn't he? He tripped, pulled on his trousers, and fumbled his shirt, buttoning the buttons wrong and having to unbutton and restart, swearing under his breath. One last trip to the basin for a palmful of water to run through his hair with a crude finger comb, and he inhaled deeply.

He listened at the door. The chatter outside had died down. Considering himself to be marginally presentable, Tom grabbed his knapsack, exhaled, and left the bedroom. The aroma of bacon, eggs, and pancakes bombarded his senses instantly, and his stomach grumbled in response. He had forgotten how hungry he was. Making his way to the dining room, off the lounge, he found Weasel seated before a plate of decadence, his napkin tied around his skinny neck. A carafe of coffee steamed on the table.

"Hope you had a good night's sleep, my boy. Maria shall be bringing in more breakfast. She is a great cook, you know."

Tom shifted his gaze in the direction of the kitchen at the mention of her name. Weasel seemed oblivious. Good, Tom thought, he intended to keep it that way.

"You slept like a log last night. When I got back early this morning, I checked in on you. I had no choice but to sleep on the couch. Fortunately, Simalala opted for the truck. Tom…Tom, are you even listening to me?"

Tom was staring at the door to the kitchen. Weasel snapped his fingers in front of him, and Tom mumbled an apology.

"Be patient, boyo. Breakfast is coming."

When Maria emerged from the kitchen with a sizzling platter of bacon and eggs, he tried unsuccessfully to avert his eyes, but Weasel caught the trail of his gaze, and he laughed.

"Looks like you are starving. Well, dig in, me boy," he said again, completely oblivious to the energy in the room.

Their secret was safe, thought Tom. He shot Maria a look that he hoped would be interpreted kindly. He wasn't sure what to do. He wanted to lift her into his arms and carry her back into the bedroom and show her that he was worthy of her love. He wanted a chance to say the right thing.

Weasel had piled his plate full and was engrossed in devouring his meal, impervious to the turmoil in Tom's head. Thankfully Maria didn't join them for breakfast and instead retreated to the kitchen. Maybe this would give Tom time to think. He piled his plate high, grateful for the distraction and small talk, as he shoved a mouthful of egg into his mouth.

After breakfast, they withdrew to the lounge, where Tom had first met Maria only a day before. As he listened to Weasel describe the events of the previous night, his mind wandered, and he recognized that he was again harboring feelings of resentment for his friend, his success, his footloose lifestyle…Maria. Why did he have Maria, too, he thought? He didn't even know her, did he? Well, certainly not like he knew her. He shook these thoughts free. Weasel was his friend. He was entitled to his success. He had never had a wife or a child, and maybe this was his way of feeling like he had family, even if she was essentially nothing more than an employee. He had to come clean with Weasel and tell him about Maria. As soon as Weasel was in the clear and this was all over, he must broach the topic.

"When will the boat arrive?" asked Tom agitatedly.

"It already did half an hour ago. Just wondering what's keeping Len so occupied?" said Weasel, nestled comfortably on the couch

Jaysus Weasel, I should have been out of here this morning, early." said Tom worried about the optics.

"I really didn't expect him to arrive so soon," said Weasel honestly. "Where are you going to go now? You might as well just stay. Besides, I've been thinking, isn't he the one that sent you to warn me anyway? And it's not a crime for you to pay me a visit, right?

Simalala is putting air in your tires, so you skip out after the formalities if you like."

Weasel pulled open the drawer of the end table beside him to reveal a packet of cigarettes and a box of cigars. He placed a thin skin between his lips, struck a match, and lit it before offering Tom one of the cigars. Tom smiled and placed it between his fingers, and leaned in to get a light from Weasel's cigarette tip.

"You have cigars now, Señor Tim?"

"You know how much I hate these bloody things, Tom. But I must keep a supply, you know, for business' sake. You understand, of course." They both laughed.

"Tim, there's a policeman here to see you," said Mooi Boetie barging in after a curt rap at the door.

"I hope you didn't greet him with a greener to the back of his head," said Tom sarcastically, earning a frown from the hefty man.

"Will you please escort him in, respectfully!" said Weasel.

A few minutes later, Leonard Johnston entered the room as Mooi Boetie stepped to the side. Weasel erupted from his seat, extending his hand to the policeman. It was a thespian-worthy performance. He had always been good at deception, acknowledged Tom as he struggled to match his enthusiasm, rising from his armchair. Maybe this explained why he wasn't cut out for this smuggling business.

"Len … Len Johnston, my, what a pleasant surprise!" said Weasel, vigorously, shaking his hand.

"Thank you, Pretty Boy," affirmed Weasel giving Mooi Boetie permission to leave and earning him a quizzical look from Len upon his departure.

"Tom, I was not expecting to see you here," said Len, slightly unnerved to find Tom here at the trading post.

"Oh, don't mind me, Len. I am more surprised to see you here. I'm just in the area to buy cattle and to pay my old pal a visit." Tom said slyly with a wink only Len could see.

Len grinned at his friend as he wiped the pool of sweat already forming on his forehead and made himself comfortable in the armchair at Weasel's behest. Weasel took his seat, and so did Tom.

Weasel attempted to maneuver the conversation.

"Trouble from one of the locals, Len? You can tell us. Hey Maria, can you bring in some coffee for our guest, love?" he shouted in the direction of the kitchen.

Maria called back affirmatively and, within seconds, arrived with a coffee tray, three cups of milk, and sugar and placed the tray on the coffee table between the couch and the armchairs. She smiled politely at Len, who nodded and again wiped his perspiring brow uncomfortably. As Maria set about serving up the coffee, Tom deemed it his responsibility to introduce her.

"This is Anna Maria Gomes," Tom said, ignoring Weasel's look of irritation as he usurped the moment as master of ceremonies.

Len gawked at Maria as she poured and handed him his coffee. She was undeniably attractive, and her self-assurance in the company of men only added to the mystique. She bowed slightly to Len but allowed the depth of her gaze to linger on Tom as she wafted out of the room.

"Well, well, who was that delightful creature, and where have you been hiding her, my dear chap," asked Len, almost forgetting why he was there to start with.

Insinuations about Maria began to fly amidst fits of laughter between the men as Len expounded on the novel idea of having a kept woman. Weasel played along, and Tom could feel the heat rising to his face and fists.

"Enough with the bullshit. Why are you here, Len? What's the purpose of your visit?"

Both men snapped in his direction. Neither had noticed that Tom had been a non-participant in their ribaldry. Even Tom was a bit taken back by his own outburst.

Len sobered quickly and pulled an envelope from his pocket. Standing, he handed it formally to Weasel as he threw Tom a sideways glance.

Weasel glanced at the document and shot up. "What? Are you serious, Len? Of all the people, you are accusing me of illegally trading gold. This is outrageous. Had it been someone else, I would not have been offended, but I thought we were friends, mate."

Len sat back down and lifted the coffee cup to his lips, and took a gulp. He urged Weasel to take a seat, and after another stage-worthy performance of manufactured outrage, Weasel sat too. Calmly Len explained that the investigation was merely protocol. He assured Weasel that he believed him to be innocent and had purposely taken his case so that he could be vindicated. Len explained how the informant was a German as Tom watched Weasel's face turn imperceptibly gray at the elucidation of betrayal. Apparently, this man had provided details on certain locations and a chip of gold as evidence.

Len drained the remainder of his coffee and, heaving a sigh, apologized once more to Weasel before exiting the outpost and rounding up the four constables who had escorted him there. Weasel maintained his show of innocence, calling after Len and his men as they drove off.

"I'm not a criminal, Len. You won't find anything. Your informant is a fraud. You'll see."

In Len's absence, Weasel sent for Mooi Boetie and the German, only to find neither was around. Tom had remained in Weasel's company, assuring him that everything would work out. He knew that Weasel had covered his tracks, and for that, he was glad. He needed to know no more about it. While they waited for the police to return, Tom filled Weasel in on Heidi, her commencement, and subsequent trip to Salisbury. He was unconsciously avoiding any discussion about Maria and was grateful that she had been elusive since Len left.

When Len returned a couple of hours later, having set his men to task, Weasel was still parading his fake bruised ego, mostly to make Len feel guilty. A forced conversation ensued about local news and gossip, while Weasel continued to play the charming host, offering the sergeant his best whiskey and an invitation to stay for dinner. This only added salt to the guilty wound that Len was already nursing, and Tom knew this was Weasel gloating. Weasel was enjoying watching Len squirm and lose his upper hand. As each constable returned to the trading post-empty-handed, Len tempered the awkward conversation with the occasional apology and well wishes for Weasel's legitimate trade business.

After a final search of the house, the tension finally crumbled when one of the policemen returned from Maria's bedroom, rubbing his head and grumbling incoherently. Apparently, when the man had begun rummaging indelicately though her trunk, she had thrown a metal brush at him and sworn at him in Portuguese.

"That's the Portuguese temper for you." laughed Weasel, and both Len and Tom had to laugh at his misfortune.

"I am sorry for all this, Weasel, but I hope you can understand that I had to follow protocol. I cannot tell you how happy I am to report your innocence. You know I would have hated to arrest you."

"Apology accepted. And for my part, I am sorry to have lost my temper with you earlier. I know you are only doing your job. So how about another drink and some dinner." insisted Weasel, losing his air of superiority, glad that the ordeal was over.

Len ordered his men back to a local police station and stayed to enjoy the pleasant hospitality at the trading post, free from inhibition and officially off duty. After a fine evening of good food, laughter, and a fair amount of drinking, Weasel drove Len back to the police station. As he stumbled out of the car, Len turned to him and said in a slur.

"I know you are involved in the business, Weasel, but I am happy that I did not have to catch you at it. As your friend, I must tell you to abandon it. It's going to get dangerous. Oh, and best rid of that German of yours."

As Len waved goodbye to them, Weasel turned to Tom and grunted some profanities.

"Don't say you told me so, Tom." insisted Weasel as he started the car. "I should have known better than to trust that bloody German."

"Where's that snitching bastard! Fumed Weasel as he pulled into the trading post, nearly running over Mooi Boetie. "He is the one who has been ratting me out!"

"What happened?" Mooi asked nervously. Weasel, despite his diminutive height, could be quite intimidating when he was angry, and Mooi Boetie had obviously seen this side of him before.

"Where is that bastard? Where's the German?"

"What's happening?" Mooi Boetie yelled as he pursued an enraged Weasel into the outpost. Tom followed to watch the circus act play out.

"Holtz is away. He said he had to visit his sister in Nyasaland. He said he's be back in a couple of weeks." said the man, stammering as he followed him into the building. Weasel turned, his eyes narrowing on Mooi Boetie.

"A couple of weeks my arse? He was plotting against the very hand which fed him this whole time. He's the snitch!" Weasel yelled. "And I hate snitches. If this had been the old country, that would be the end of him."

"I'll take care of him, Tim," said Mooi Boetie as he turned to leave.

"Jaysus, don't kill the man. Just rough him up a bit and tell him to never show his face around here again."

Mooi Boetie looked at Tom standing just within the shop door. Boetie gritted his teeth and made his way to the door, claiming he'd find him and skin the snitcher alive. Tom stood aside as the man pushed past him, slamming the shop door behind him.

"You know that rugged ox will literally skin Holtz alive?" Tom said with a smirk.

"No. He will only dislocate something…maybe crack a couple of his ribs and send him crying down the river."

"Unless he's in on the scam."

"No! Definitely not. He may be a brute, but he damn near saved my life umpteen times. That's why I rolled him into this deal in the first place. He might seem rough around the edges, but Mooi Boetie is a decent man …I trust him. Look, Tom, I am sorry about all this. I never meant for you to be involved. Spend another night or two here so we can catch up without having anyone breathing down our necks. What do you say?"

Tom accepted. Maybe if they settled into a more comfortable routine, and talked about all times, he might be able to pluck up the courage to bring up Maria. She had avoided them since breakfast, and Tom assumed that she either felt betrayed or was full of regret. They took dinner at the beer hall that night, where Weasel introduced Tom to some of the locals. Maria obviously did not join them. In the company of these strange men, there was no opportune moment to turn the conversation towards Maria. Besides, he feared that even innocently mentioning her name would drive them into a lewd commentary at her expense and that he couldn't bear. Back at the trading post later, Weasel graciously offered Tom his room again, but he declined.

"As long as you don't mind, mate. I don't have another bedroom, so the couch is the next best thing. Unless you want to shack up with Maria." Weasel said with a wink as he took himself to bed, not noticing the tinge of blush arise in his friend's cheeks."

"Nah, couch is superb, Weasel. Thanks. And Simalala could sleep under the stars every night. He's happy as anything out on the truck."

"Alright then," said Weasel in drunken sleepiness as he made his exit.

Tom took off his boots and shirt and spread out the blanket Weasel had left him on the couch, allowing enough drag to pull the remaining half over his body. He flicked off the light. Lying in the dark, he wondered if Maria would come to him again. He searched for her eyes in the darkness, for the patter of naked feet or the scent of her skin. But she never came. He almost began to wonder if their night together a figment of his imagination had been.

The following day Maria greeted him with a warm smile as she brought in their breakfast. This time she joined them but remained quiet, sipping her coffee with her eyes glued to the book in her right hand. Tom and Weasel chatted about their antics as impressionable boys growing up in Ireland. Every so often, Tom would catch Maria peering at him over her book, but then she would quickly avert her eyes.

Weasel had no interest in engaging her in the conversation. He never asked her to leave, but he didn't go out of his way either to include her. Weasel was enjoying Tom's undivided attention. He had missed his friend and all the memories they had shared over a span of

over two decades. He wanted to enjoy every minute of it, not knowing when their paths might again cross. Weasel spouted on with tale
after tale in true Irish fashion while Maria and Tom were subjugated
to stolen glances and short interjections. One thing was for certain,
their night together had not been a fantasy.

After breakfast, the men went on a tour of the little town. Weasel
was anxious to show him how much had changed since Tom was last
here. The Depression hadn't touched the place. In fact, Weasel's trading post had helped propel improvements and development. It hadn't
been much of a place to start with, but a few houses had cropped up
since Tom's last visit, and the beer hall and civic building had been
refreshed with new paint and added outbuildings. It was evident that
Weasel and his business had been an asset here, despite his illicit
activities. Tom couldn't help but be proud of him, this scrappy lad
from Donegal.

Maria had promised them a special dinner that night. She was preparing a true Portuguese dish called cabidela, for which Weasel raved.

"She is a lovely cook," said Weasel reiterated as they returned to
his place. "Between you and me, I honestly don't know what I'd do
without her. I know I give her the cold shoulder sometimes, but it's
because I like her, I think, and I know she has no feelings for me. But
it's the closest I'll ever get to having a family, Tom. Maybe I'll become
like a comfortable old sock, and someday she'll change her mind."
Weasel laughed with an edge of honesty.

Tom was deflated. How could he bring up Maria now? It would
only seem like a betrayal. Purposefully Tom turned the conversation
to Demberra. They discussed Tom's dealings with Bradley and the
risk he had leveraged. Weasel imparted some insight on Bradley,
which he had exhumed through his business circles; notably, he was
a cheat and womanizer and not to be trusted. This was beginning to
sound like the consensus.

Dinner was, as promised, a culinary delight. Maria had expertly
stewed chunks of kudu in red wine and served it over a bed of rice
with roasted yams. They all drank Spanish wine as a compliment to
the cook, as they laughed about their cultural traditions, and Weasel

bemoaned the blandness of Irish food, considering her good cooking. Maria lit up when she spoke about her family and her traditions. This was the most she had spoken in their joint company, and Tom found it comforting to see her smile and relish in happy memories after having witnessed first-hand her deep sense of loss and isolation. Weasel did not notice the way they held each other's gaze a little too long for mere acquaintances, nor did he witness Tom grasp her hand under the table. It had not been a dream. He had real feelings for this woman.

Maria retired graciously after dinner, allowing the two friends some time alone. It would have been the perfect opportunity for Tom to bring up the subject, but how could he now? How could he hurt Weasel like that? Maybe Maria would come to love him. Weasel had no one after all, and Tom had Heidi to take care of. He had been foolish to think anything could come of it anyway. He resolutely compartmentalized Maria to a part of his heart that must stay sealed, and he drowned out any thoughts of her as they laughed and drank their way through another two bottles of Spanish wine.

"Why don't you take my room tonight, lad," said Weasel jovially, swaying a little from side to side.

"No, not at all. Besides, I like your couch," said Tom protesting. He wanted Weasel tucked away in his room tonight if he was going to have the courage to do what he had to do.

"As long as you're sure." laughed Weasel, slapping him on the arm. "I'll be off then." Tom nodded as Weasel disappeared down the hallway. He waited until he heard the door close, and Weasel's body hit the bed with a thud. He stood waiting in silence until the house was still, and then tiptoeing like a fugitive, he made his way down the hallway, palm to the wall as he felt his way in the dark.

Standing before Maria's door, he could feel his heart beating in his ear. A faint light outlined the door frame. She was awake. He twisted the knob gently and slipped in. The room was dimly lit by a bedside lamp that illuminated the brass bedframe and kaleidoscope quilt that Maria lay beneath. She was fast asleep. Her fragrance hung in the air, and he allowed himself to imbibe it; sweet and spicy. A music box delicately painted with a forest scene sat by her bedside, along with the book she was reading earlier, lying open on the page. A carved wooden trunk that looked like it had been in her family for generations and had been the subject of a certain constable's downfall stood majestically at the foot of the bed. Bright silk scarves in orange and red hues framed the window and rippled gently against the breeze through the half-open window. The moon was full again, and it threw a silvery glow across Maria's face. She looked so peaceful. He just wanted to wrap her in his arms and share in her tranquility.

His whole body ached for her. He approached the bed and, leaning over her, scraped his lips gently on her forehead. Her eyelashes fluttered open against his throat.

"I have been waiting for you for many hours. I thought you wouldn't come… I fell asleep."

Tom knelt by her bedside as she lifted her head. They stared into each other's eyes and said nothing. Tom ran his fingers through her long black hair, and closing his eyes, he found her lips. An internal struggle between his body and mind erupted. He pulled away abruptly, releasing Maria, and stood.

"I am leaving in the morning, Maria. I just came to say goodbye," he said more abruptly than he intended as he moved quickly to the door, afraid of his own will. He turned and soaked her in one last time. She was sitting up in bed, beautiful and silent. He had injured her.

"Thomas?" she whispered

"It's for the best. Goodbye, Maria."

Tom clenched his jaw and, avoiding eye contact, pulled open her door and quickly shut it behind him. Standing silently in the hallway, he could hear her muffled sobs. He wanted to comfort her. He wanted to protect her and tell her everything would be fine. He wanted her more than he had wanted anything for as long as he could remember, but he couldn't have her. He punched the wall as he made his way back to the lounge in the dark.

CHAPTER 9

RUNAWAY

By six in the morning, the men were ready to depart. They wanted to get to Simalala's village before nightfall. Considering what had transpired the night before, Tom was anxious to get on the road, buy his cattle and return to Demberra, and try to put Maria from his mind. Simalala had filled the petrol tank and loaded up the truck bed with supplies of coffee, grains, fresh bread, nuts, tobacco, soaps, and gifts for Heidi and Simalala's family, courtesy of Weasel. Since Maria apparently wasn't awake, breakfast was illusive, but Weasel had made a generous pot of coffee early that morning for their journey. Simalala, as always, declined as he perceived the black liquid to be nothing but evil, tasting like sour umfazi melek[9]. The two Irishmen laughed at his disdain for the stuff, enjoying their strong coffee from a large flask outside the trading post.

Weasel asked if Tom wished to bid his Spanish maiden farewell. Tom declined, albeit with a heavy heart, proclaiming it would be selfish and unfair to wake her up this early for a goodbye. Once Simalala had safely secured everything in the trunk bed with ropes, Tom took his old friend in a warm embrace.

---

[9]   Woman's milk

"It was great seeing you after such a long time, Tom," said Weasel, a little teary-eyed. "I must make a trip to Demberra one of these days. It's been too long. Maybe when Heidi gets home again."

"That would be grand," said Tom. "I'll be looking forward to it. Take care of Maria Weasel, she's a good woman."

Weasel grinned and waved like a schoolboy as they pulled out of the trading post. After the dust cloud, kicked up by the truck, had completely obscured the vehicle from view, he retreated into the shop, recognizing pangs of hunger brewing.

"Time to wake Maria and have her whip up some breakfast, I think," he said cheerfully to himself.

After a few minutes in the store making some mental calculations on inventory, he retreated down the hallway and back into his house. It was unusually quiet. He had expected to be bombarded by the familiar smell of bacon and toast, but there was none. Usually, by this time, Maria had already made breakfast and was in the store prepping merchandise for the day. Farmers are early risers, and the trading post typically saw a fair amount of activity by seven am. He called for her, but nothing. At her bedroom door knocking, he was also met with silence. After a full minute of rapping at her door, he barged in. The door was not locked.

"Bloody hell, she's gone! Lock, stock and bloody barrel, her enormous trunk and all, Jaysus, Mary, and holy Saint Joseph!" he was dumbfounded for a moment and then swiftly turned and yelled down the passageway at his house servant.

"Where is she? Where is Dona[10]?"

"She has left, Bwana." replied the man nervously arriving at his side, even more, diminutive than Weasel.

He shifted his eyes from Weasel's intense glare to the floor. Speaking quickly now and determinedly, the African explained how Maria had left before dawn, paying two strong young Muntu, who had been hanging around the beer hall, to carry her enormous trunk. She was apparently headed north.

---

[10]   Madam

"All she said was that she had to leave. She couldn't live here anymore. And she had to hurry."

Weasel undid the first two buttons of his shirt as sweat beaded on his forehead and began to run down his face. He had never mistreated her, he assured himself. She had a good life here. Why would she leave? And where the hell would she go to anyway? And then, like a cloud shifting to reveal the blinding sun behind it, he understood. It was Tom. Tom was headed in that direction, and then he would veer off to Simalala's village. She had left to meet up with Tom.

"That big sweet-talking bastard! He just barges in here and steals my girl." Weasel shouted at the African, who merely nodded in agreement and shuffled back down the hallway, leaving Weasel to de-escalate his anger alone.

"Well, good riddance," he said under his breath, half in anger and half in sheer respect for the man. He had missed the romance that had been right under his nose the whole time.

"Be careful what you ask for, Thomas, me lad." he scolded under his breath, half seriously and half in jest. Those Portuguese women have quite the temper, let me tell you. you could have met your match boyo." He smiled to himself and closed the door to Maria's room. He had already conceded long ago that Maria would never settle down with him. It had only been a matter of time. How lively Demberra would now be, he thought, with two hot tempers and one headstrong teenager. He laughed out loud to himself and walked to the dining room, and called to the African servant.

"Madala[11], we don't need any umfazis, do we? Now go make breakfast for me, will you? I'm starving." The old man's face was wrinkled in confusion as he tottered off to the kitchen. He had never made breakfast before.

* * *

---

[11]   Old man

Tom and Simalala were silent as the truck bumped along the dirt road for a couple of miles. Tom was consumed by thoughts of Maria, no matter how hard he tried to push them from his mind.

"Bwana, you act like a man with no tongue. I know you don't like leaving the umfazis behind," said Simalala in a mildly scolding tone, not wishing to endure this agitated silence much more.

Tom rolled his eyes. "Mind your own business."

Simalala was not deterred. "You can take her if you want. She is not Bwana Weasel's umfazis. Then her parents will have no choice but to give her to you because she will be second-hand. They cannot sell a second-hand woman."

"You're crazy," mumbled Tom dismissively. "This is the practice of my people."

"Well, it's not that easy for white men, Simalala. Besides, I couldn't accept that. For me, it's one man, one woman."

"If so, then better reason to take the woman, no," stated Simalala with affirmation.

Tom tightened his grip on the steering wheel and shrugged angrily at Simalala, waving away his commentary. He reached across him to retrieve a cigar from the glove box when Simalala grabbed his hand and yelled.

"Bwana, on the mgwagwa[12] look, your woman."

Tom saw Maria's frame come into view through the dust as he skidded the truck to a halt. He watched as the windshield wipers cleared his view to reveal a familiar petite woman wearing a pair of linen slacks and a frilly white blouse mostly covered by a form-fitting waistcoat. Her long black hair was tied in the back with a red ribbon, and she wore a black tigerdoe hat strapped loosely under her chin to shield her face from the sun. She was ready for a bullfight, or at least she was dressed for one. One hand rested on her hips as she pulled back her hat and squinted at the truck. Two strapping young African men were resting in the shade of a fig tree nearby, having

---

[12] Road

second thoughts about the job they had undertaken, namely carrying Maria's trunk for the last three miles.

Tom turned off the ignition and climbed out of his seat. As he made his way to meet her on the side of the road, he called out.

"Dear God, Maria. What are you doing here?

"It took you long enough to get here, Señor Tom," she said, exasperated, her hands still on her hips.

I didn't know we were going to a fancy-dress party. You look like a matador, Maria." said Tom teasingly as he reached her.

I've been walking and waiting for you since early this morning." Maria blurted out, thrusting a punch into his stomach that took the wind out of him.

"I suppose I deserved that," Tom said carefully

"Well, I have left Señor Tim. I want to go with you," she stated decidedly, placing her hat squarely on her head as if there would be no further negotiations.

Tom pulled her into him and kissed her, lifting her off the ground.

"You know I didn't want to leave you. I just didn't want to hurt Weasel. But I can't fight this anymore. Especially if you've left." he declared, holding her close to his chest.

"Tom. I just want you, nothing else. I want to be with you."

Tom kissed her again while the two Africans began to clap enthusiastically from the shade of the tree. Simalala abruptly motioned to them and rattled out some orders in Lozi, and the young men quickly scrambled to their feet and gratefully hoisted Maria's heavy wooden chest into the back of the truck, taking off in the other direction before the woman could change her mind.

Taking his cue, Simalala vacated his seat and jumped into the back of the truck beaming in righteousness. Tom threw him a look as he opened the door for Maria and helped her into the truck.

Maria had an uncanny way of making herself comfortable. That was part of her appeal, her unapologetically free spirit. For this reason, Tom was curious to see how she would handle Simalala's village.

Not many whites had ventured this far into the bush. It should be entertaining, at the very least, he thought, smiling to himself.

Their conversation at first was as uncomfortable as they had both anticipated. Maria explained her decision to leave Weasel and admitted that although she cared for the man, she wasn't in love with him and never would be. She confessed that she had known the night before that Tom would never betray his friend, so she knew she had to leave.

They both agreed to settle things with Weasel, the first opportunity they had. With that temporarily resolved, their conversation devolved into laughter as she explained how she was able to convince two young men, clearly nursing a hangover, to convey her enormous trunk for miles down a dusty road.

"You don't say no to a Portuguese woman Señor Tom," she said cheekily.

"I'm learning that quickly," he said with a grin.

"…And it's Thomas Edward Sutton, not Señor Tom from now, alright?"

"I know, Thomas Edward Sutton. I shall call you Thomas," she said, reaching over and placing a gentle kiss on his cheek.

She made him feel young again, even like a small child. He had been the caregiver for so long, it was comforting to be cared for and scolded. He felt like an adolescent who had just received his first love letter or stolen a kiss behind the parish church. He reached across the seat and grabbed her hand, clasping it in his. He was glad she had been braver than him.

By late morning they had traveled a fair distance, stopping only once to check the overheated radiator and to relieve themselves in the bush by the side of the road. At a specific location, almost indistinguishable from Maria, Tom veered the car off the road and into the bush. He stopped the truck, and Simalala jumped from the flatbed and made his way to the front of the vehicle to guide Tom the rest of the way.

"Simalala, I can barely see with all the Gozi[13] covering the windshield," Tom yelled out the side window as he maneuvered the truck slowly and steadily toward Simalala's waving hand. Maria shielded her eyes with her hands more than once as the car pushed through a thick bush and hobbled over motionless tree trunks haphazardly strewn across their path.

The car jerked as the decomposing tree bark crushed under the weight of the tires, and Maria had to wonder if Tom had a backup plan if this car decided to expire right here in this place. Every now and then, Tom would glance over at her and give her hand a squeeze in reassurance.

The journey through the valley brought them intimately close to wildlife, as each unassuming antelope would dart from their path at the hum of the approaching engine. Maria looked out her window with delight, watching a herd of glorious slender, long-necked Oribi stare at her inquisitively from a safer distance.

As the dense bush subsided and gave way to open land, they were granted a panoramic view of endless scenery. Simalala, now back in the truck, pointed out each animal and patch of a bush like a tour guide. Seemingly endless herds of Cape buffalo grazed in the valley, with herds of zebra and antelope in toe. The croak of the male wildebeests, like loud frogs, resounded in the open space. Animals lounged lazily in the sun, only scattering when they heard the rumble of the truck engine in the distance. Barely discernable by the naked eye was a pride of seven lions, nestled on higher ground on the other side of the valley, camouflaged under a lone tree surrounded by tall grass. Tom cut the engine for a moment and pulled his binoculars from the glove box, and showed Maria.

Maria was mesmerized. She had been near the bush before and had seen some of Africa's wildness, but never like this. To their right, Tom saw a majestic black sable bull inch out of the protection of the Gozi. For a moment, the animal stood royally tall. Tom placed his finger to his lips and pointed. Maria's eyes followed until they landed

---

[13]   Thick bush

on the awesome creature. Then like arrows being shot from the darkness, twenty ferocious wild dogs appeared out of what seemed like thin air and lurched at the bull, surrounding him in a semi-circle. The sable bolted as the dogs had strategized, and they closed off his exit with their fan-like chase as they continued to close in until they eventually pounced on the rear of the running buck. As they tackled the enormous animal, bringing him to the ground, the sable tried to stagger once more to his feet in a last-ditch effort. He took one robust swing and rammed his curved horns at the nearest bitch, killing the animal with a loud yelp. But this lunge had cost the sable all his strength, causing him to collapse to the ground once more with one horn skewering a dead dog and weighting him to the earth.

He was outnumbered on the ground as the entire pack of wild dogs dug their razor-sharp teeth into his flesh, tearing at it mercilessly as his life began to ebb away. One of the wild dogs leaped at the sable's throat, digging its teeth into the animal as it groaned loudly.

"Make them stop!" Maria screamed in desperation.

Tom knew the sable would soon be out of his misery, leaving nothing behind but a carcass, shredded skin, and bones for these hyenas to scrape later. This was the way of the wild, as gruesome as it was to behold.

"Please, God, please make it stop," Maria screamed again, tugging at Tom's sleeve imploringly.

He quickly turned the key in the ignition and revved the engine. That was successful enough to disturb the proceedings and buy him time to pull his Colt 38 from the glove box and exit the truck, Simalala at his rear. As the dogs scattered, Tom moved cautiously towards the dying sable, still struggling to lift his head off the ground, immobilized by the added burden of the dead dog impaled on his horns.

The pain and vulnerability in the sable's big eyes pleaded with Tom. Taking the cue, Tom took a position behind its stuck head, pointed his gun behind the animal's ear, and pulled the trigger. The sound of the shot reverberated loudly in the open space. The pack of dogs panicked and bolted to safety, placing a decent distance between themselves and the invader as they watched Tom return to his vehicle.

Simalala and Tom climbed into the truck, and it quickly jerked forward. Maria stifled sobs and drew herself close to Tom, hiding her eyes. As the car began to pick up speed, Tom glanced back in the rearview mirror. The dogs had returned as he had predicted and were devouring the sable. At least the animal was no longer in misery, he thought.

As they drove through the long valley, surrounded by Mutemo[14] on either side, they soon came upon a river stream that fed the village. They were close. Tom took this opportunity to describe Simalala's village and give Maria a brief history of the Lozi and how his village had survived on this water resource. Within minutes they were greeted by a crowd of smiling black men, women, and children, all wearing nothing but moochies[15] exposing their upper torsos entirely. Maria blushed, earning a grin from Tom.

About fifty dried grass huts of various sizes were erected spaciously in the vast clearing, with a rude wooden fence encircling them. Some villagers remained by their huts or were too far out in the field beyond to notice their arrival, but most had come to meet the truck and escort them in.

Simalala's father was the headman of this village and answered directly to Chief Litia. He was affectionately called Old Mamba by his son and close relatives, but Tom preferred to call him Black Mamba because, despite his advanced age, his wrath and agility rivaled the deadliest of snakes, the Black Mamba. Simalala found the nickname suited to his warrior father, for at seventy years of age, he still ruled with authority and would not be crossed.

It was no surprise that when they pulled up their truck in front of the hut, it was the most magnificent one of them all. The grand abode of Black Mamba, head man to the chief himself, was three times the size of any of the neighboring huts, and although the entire

---

[14] Impassable bush
[15] Loin cloth that stretches between legs and is tied around the waist

dwelling was thatched like the rest, his home's foundation was poured concrete and featured an arch and stairs at its entrance.

By now, the sun was at its high peak. Strands of Maria's black hair had come loose and clung to the perspiration on her forehead. She had long since abandoned the waistcoat and hat, and even her blouse had become sticky and more transparent with perspiration.

As they disembarked in front of a hut, the local women surrounded her, staring at her with their mouths agape. It soon became obvious that it was not her that they were enthralled with, but her brassiere, whose outline could be seen through her sheer white blouse and whose strap one brave young girl had snapped impudently from behind.

Maria clung to Tom's arm to escape the unwanted adoration as a formidable old man engulfed Tom's palm in his and shook it firmly. It was a European custom that the old man adored. Simalala stood at Tom's side, beaming with pride.

"I see you, Bwana Tom," he said with authority and genuine friendliness, shaking his hand.

"I see you too, Mamba," Tom said, returning the gesture with a big smile.

"I see you, Simalala." said the old man.

Unlike Tom and his father, Simalala did not shake hands with his father but instead bowed in respect and clapped his left palm with his right-hand finger, as was the custom. After acknowledging his son, Mamba then turned to face Maria, and his grin increased, revealing his yellowish teeth.

"You have umfazis now after a long time, Bwana Sutton. Good!" he said, looking at Tom with satisfaction.

Tom quickly introduced Maria. Mamba made sure to exchange greetings with her as was customary in European culture, where women were granted a level of respect that he could not comprehend. Here in his village, the women were only of value with respect to their husbands and fathers. They existed to attend to men's needs, give them healthy lines of progeny, and keep the home. But the old man smiled respectively and bowed slightly to Maria before ushering them both into the hut whilst barking orders to his servants to prepare Tom's hut for his stay.

After some tea, English style, as was customary when Tom visited, Tom walked Maria, followed by her throng of adoring fans, to his guest hut. It was nearly as impressive as Mamba's, without the reception area. They passed through a thick-lined Zebra skin door into a large, freshly cleaned space. On the left side of the hut lay a large Kudu skin sprawled across the floor. Tom's two wooden canvas folding chairs had been brought in from his truck and placed next to a beautifully carved driftwood table. A flask and bowl of fresh mangoes had been placed on it for their welcome. Tom's bags had been stored neatly in the corner of the room, near another carved table that held a kerosene gas lamp. Blankets and pillows had been carefully laid out on an intricately woven grass mat in the back of the hut. This was presumably their bed for the night, she surmised.

Seeing that she was getting accustomed to the space, Tom excused himself to go and meet with Mamba, urging Maria to rest and make herself comfortable until he returned. It didn't take long to familiarize herself with the hut, and then she paced back and forth, waiting for Tom, filled with a mixture of uncertainty and excitement. It had been bold of her to leave the relative comfort and security of Weasel's trading post. Was she sure about life with this Thomas Edward Sutton? Then her eyes settled on the grass mat bed in the corner of the hut, and the realization that she would spend the night there in the warm embrace of her lover made her shiver with glorious anticipation. She only wished she had her trunk, so she could change out of these sweaty, dusty clothes, but she was too afraid to venture outside for fear of the adoring village women.

A few hundred yards away, Tom was receiving the royal treatment as Mamba's business guest. There was a formality to these proceedings. Upon arrival, the men always indulged themselves in local beer, some salted fish, fresh mangoes, and figs while conversing about the current laws and regulations. Mamba and Simalala smoked extremely potent Dagga[16] throughout the meeting. Tom indulged lightly, only to be polite, trying his best not to inhale and wishing he could smoke a good cigar instead.

Maria was becoming restless. Maybe if she peaked her head out of the hut, she could catch one of Mamba's servant's attention and then fetch her trunk. She gently pulled back the skin to search for help, and no less than ten feet away sat a huddle of women waiting to pounce. She quickly closed the skin and retreated into the hut irritated.

Now nearly suffocating from the obnoxious smell of Dagga, Tom graciously excused himself, using Maria as an excuse to escape the smoke-filled hut. He had satisfied the formalities of his arrival. Approaching the hut, he could see that a crowd had formed outside, and he suddenly felt concerned for Maria. He pushed past the crowd of mostly women and barged into the hut, nearly knocking Maria over.

"Thomas, I am so glad you are here. The women outside scare me." Maria said, clinging to his neck.

"What happened, Maria?" he asked softly, stroking her hair. "Those naked women outside. They have been standing there ever since I came, Thomas. They won't leave me alone."

Tom stifled a laugh, which earned him a frown from Maria. "Can you please tell them to go away?" she implored

"If that is what you want, then of course."

"Yes, it is! That is most definitely what I want!" she said defiantly with her hands on her hips.

She listened at the doorway, peeling back the skin slightly, as Tom gently scolded the women in Fanagalo, an informal language of Zulu-based pidgin, other African dialects, English, and Afrikaans, that he's picked up over the years. When he reentered the hut, he brought a timid young girl with him. She hid behind him as if she was afraid of Maria.

"All of them have taken their leave. All but one. This is Simalala's sister, Mwangala."

---

[16]   Marijuana

Maria moved her eyes from Tom to the young girl who stood behind him, almost completely naked and looking embarrassedly at her feet.

Tom cleared his throat and gestured to her. "She has brought you a gift, Maria."

"That is very sweet of the girl, what is it?" said Maria tentatively Tom bent down to the girl's eye level and spoke to her in Fanagalo. She nodded.

The girl was no more than seventeen years of age, Maria thought. The girl revealed an unrolled loincloth, a virgin moochi sewn out of Zebra skin. She bowed as she presented it to Maria. Not wanting to upset the girl, Maria graciously accepted it and bowed in return. When the girl did not budge from her position, Maria turned to face Tom, confused.

"Well, now it is your turn to give her a present. It is the local culture," Tom stated, shrugging his shoulders.

"Well, what does she want, Thomas?"

Tom leaned down and asked the girl in her native tongue.

The girl answered, pointing at Maria, and Tom started to laugh. "She wants you, er…brassiere Maria," Tom said with a childish grin.

"What?" Maria yelled as she placed a protective hand on her chest. The girl looked like she would cry.

"Tell her I will give her a new one from my trunk," Maria said, pointing at the door. "If someone can get me my trunk, I'll give her a nice fresh one."

He obligatorily conveyed the message to the girl, who only frowned and shook her head no, pointing again at Maria's shirt.

"I am afraid she wants the one you have on Maria. And I am sorry about this, but if you don't give the girl what she wants, then we will both be in trouble. They will consider you rude. And disrespect is not tolerated. Our stay will not be pleasant after that, I assure you." he said emphatically.

Maria sighed. There was no winning this fight.

"Please have her turn around," she said as she started to unbutton her blouse. Tom signaled to the girl, and she obliged.

"Wait! You better wear this. After you take that off and give the girl her present, I'll be in trouble." he said as he winked and pulled one of his vests from his bag, tossing it to her.

Maria took the vest, thankfully, and began to unbutton her blouse. He closed his eyes as she threw the blouse on the bed mat and removed the brassiere. He was afraid of his own impulses, especially in a stranger's presence.

"I'm decent," said Maria coyly after she pulled his vest over her head.

He opened his eyes. She stood before him in his oversized vest, her firm subtle breasts pressed to the fabric. She held her brassiere out to the girl like a reluctant offering.

The girl was completely aware of the flirtation and sexual tension hanging in the room and grabbed the brassiere from Tom with gusto. She placed it on her chest and turned her back to Maria, indicating that she should fasten it for her.

"Well, she obviously wants to wear it … right now." Tom laughed as Maria looked to him for guidance.

Maria rolled her eyes at him and obliged the girl, fastening the undergarment on the tightest setting as the girl examined her own bosom, admiring the way it looked in this new contraption. She bowed to Maria and mumbled something indistinguishable to Tom.

"She thanks you for the gift, and she wants to return the gesture by teaching you how to wear the moochi that she gave you." Maria's cheeks flushed scarlet.

"Please tell her to thank you, but I can manage on my own," she said with exasperation, mustering up a smile and a nod for the girl.

Satisfied with the exchange, the girl escaped out the front of the hut to show off her brassiere to the other young women who were milling around in anticipation at a respectable distance from their hut as promised.

As soon as the skin flap closed, Maria threw herself at Tom. Her firm, unbridled breasts pressed against him, and he could feel every fiber of his body respond. She wrapped her arms around his neck and kissed him deeply. His hands reached up her bare back and into her thick hair, loose and wild at the nape of her neck. Her stomach grumbled against him. He pulled back, shaking his head with a smile.

"Maria, you're hungry. You probably haven't eaten anything all day. Let me fetch some biltong[17] and a loaf of bread from the truck. Maria silenced him by pulling him back into her again and kissing him.

"Woman, if you can disarm me in my old vest, I will be helpless if I see you in that moochi."

He reluctantly pried himself from her arms and promised he'd be right back with some food and her trunk. He returned ten minutes later, backing into the hut and dragging the trunk in front of him, with a bag on his back filled with food. As he closed the skin flap and turned to face her, she stood in front of him wearing nothing more than the Zebra loin cloth.

"Are you disarmed, Thomas?" she said in a low, sultry voice. He devoured her with his eyes, taking in every inch of her luscious mocha skin.

He approached her slowly, never dropping eye contact, and he placed his hands around her bare waist, scooping her up into an embrace.

"I will not be responsible for holding myself back." "Please don't, my Thomas. I ache for you."

Tom lay Maria roughly on the blanket spread across the grass mat. He leaned back for a moment to look at her perfect body. Her voluptuous breasts stood ready for him. She rushed to unbutton his shirt as he fumbled with his belt, throwing it across the room. Her hands massaged his bare chest as she pulled him into her, skin against skin. He kissed her deeply while one hand fondled her breasts and the other struggled to release his waistband. Maria reached down to assist him, unzipping his slacks and reaching beneath the zipper to touch him. He wriggled his way out of his trousers and undershorts in a fury. They were joined at the lips, and their naked bodies were now entwined as they felt each other's bodies. The only thing sepa-

---

[17] Dried meat

rating him from all of her was that loin cloth that still shrouded her secret place.

He kissed her from neck to navel, sending shivers through her body. When he reached the moochi, he tugged at one of the string ties with his teeth and pulled back the flap revealing his prize. He kissed her again and again as she writhed beneath him. This time he didn't wait for permission. He thrust himself into her as she gasped with pleasure. Together they moved, locked in an embrace of skin and sweet perspiration like the rhythmic gyration of a rocking boat, rising and falling with the waves of the ocean. When their panting finally quelled, they fell in a depleted mound of interwoven limbs.

"I love you, Thomas," Maria whispered in Tom's ear as he lay naked and bereft in her arms. He pulled her tightly into his chest and kissed her.

CHAPTER 10

BLACK DOT

As pigments of red and orange sunlight seeped through the cracks of the skin doorway, Tom slowly opened one eye. He could smell the earthiness of the wood fire outside the hut and the aroma of fresh coffee, thanks to one of Mamba's servants, designated to tend to the needs of his special guests. He loved the mornings in Africa, especially when he was in the bush, and all of it was so tangible. And this morning, especially, was full of opportunity. With the formalities complete, today, he could discuss his purchase of the cattle with Mamba and begin the trek home with his new herd. When Tom emerged, fully dressed, the servant handed him a cup of coffee in a tin cup, fresh from the fire kettle.

Thanking him, Tom took the coffee and pulled a cigar from his pocket, a great accompaniment to his morning brew. After a few generous puffs, he sauntered over to the truck and sat down on the running board to begin his morning shaving routine. He was already lathered up and busy sweeping the razor on his stubble when Maria emerged from the hut dressed today in sensible slacks, a short-sleeved blouse, boots, and her hair neatly braided in a thick plait and twisted into a bun. She smiled and placed a generous kiss on his cheek, avoiding his shaving cream. He retaliated with a full-mouth kiss, bestowing her with a white soapy mustache. She laughed.

After a hearty breakfast of eggs and freshly caught fish, and more coffee, the two took a leisurely stroll through the village. Bare-breasted women sorted through baskets of maize and gutted fresh fish while their naked children played nearby. Only a few men remained in the village, mostly old men, as the bulk had already left at dawn to fish and hunt. Maria soon discovered that she was a local celebrity, Mwangala waved at her from a hut up ahead, proudly showing off Maria's brassiere. Thereafter a small crowd of young girls and children followed them on their tour, which Maria came to find less threatening and more amusing.

Maria's feelings for Tom were apparent, already demonstrated by her willingness to leave everything behind. He, however, wasn't sure that he could offer her what she wanted right now in her life, which was likely a husband. But he couldn't deny the bond that had formed between them, and it wasn't just physical attraction. He was charmed by her stubbornness and self-confidence and how that strength could co-exist in that same small body with her tenderness and childlike naivete. He felt at peace when he was with her and didn't have to put on any act. It was refreshing. Time would sort things out, he thought as they walked hand in hand, chattering, without any awkwardness filling the gap between them.

When they returned to his hut, Tom employed the aid of two of Mamba's men to help load their luggage and other sundry items, and he left Maria with a quick kiss and promise not to be too long. This morning he would meet with Mamba and execute the trans-action on the cattle for which he had come. This had always been the protocol here in the village; at least one day of social interaction and hospitality always had to precede the business transaction. That's the way the old man liked it. As soon as he was escorted inside and seated, Tom jumped straight to business. He was anxious to get back to Demberra.

"So how many cattle do you have to sell, Mamba? I can take a larger amount this time."

"None." came Mamba's succinct response as he looked at Tom firmly and puffed on his Dagga.

The curt reply hit Tom like a bullet, so he repeated himself, believing the old man must have heard him wrong.

"None." The old man stated again with an oddly self-satisfied grin that made Tom angry.

"None? What do you mean, Mamba. You knew I would be coming. Did you sell them to someone else? All of them? Did you?" Tom said, rising now in anger and desperation, realizing what this meant for Demberra.

Simalala was also bewildered at his father's response but remained silent.

"They pay me well." said the old man indignantly.

"They paid you well. Who paid you well? Asked Tom looking to Simalala for answers. Simalala only clenched his fists but stayed rooted next to his father, just as perplexed as Tom was.

Mamba placed aside his Dagga and stood to meet Tom's frame. "A mampara[18] from Livingstone. He buys two hundred and fifty yesterday morning. And he pays me to double, Bwana."

"I thought we had an agreement Mamba," said Tom gritting his teeth. It had taken him four years to work out this arrangement, and there had been an unspoken guarantee that Mamba wouldn't sell to any other whites. He had proven himself trustworthy and had always made a fair deal with the old man. Tom was so upset that he declared their agreement to be null and void from that point on. He began to mutter incoherent words under his breath and ran a hand through his hair in frustration while Mamba and Simalala began to wriggle uncomfortably in their seats.

Simalala threw Tom a look, trying to de-escalate the tension and hoping to diffuse Tom's temper a notch.

"How much did they give you?" said Tom finally, attempting to get to the bottom of it and not wishing to completely lose his temper and put himself and Maria's lives in jeopardy.

Mamba reached for a rusty biscuit tin on the table between them and handed it to Tom

---

[18] Fool or a useless person.

"Open it and see. They pay me paper money. No evil can steal this. See ten-pound notes."

Tom's memory was jolted back to an incident Simalala had conveyed to him back in their days in the mine, the same story he and Charlie had discussed only days before. Apparently, seven or eight years before, a young white man had come to procure his cattle. The old man had been taken by the foreigner, and treated him to the utmost hospitality. But in his gullibility, he had shown the man a metal latched lunchbox full of hundreds of Edward V11 1902 sovereign gold coins, presumably given to him by Chief Lewanika himself in payment for his bravery in the great war with the Matebele. Mamba hadn't really understood the value of his fortune other than recognizing that gold itself had value and importance. White men's coins all looked pretty much the same to him.

But the white man, after one cursory look at the coins, was fully aware of their value on the black market, especially given the predicted rise in the value of gold. In the middle of the night, he and an accomplice took off with Mamba's sixty-pound treasure box, killing two of his servants in the process. That was the reason it had taken years for Mamba to trust another white man. It was only because of Simalala that he had even agreed to meet Tom in the first place. Henceforth Mamba had only ever sold to Tom. Tom lifted the lid off the biscuit tin and stared at the roll of paper within. He removed the roll and spread the notes across the table. *"Tenth Year, Britain's Prize-Winning Condensed Milk."*

The labels bore a photo of King George V, with a large number 10 emblazed across the front. Mamba would have been acquainted with images of King George. After Chief Lewanika attended the coronation of his predecessor Edward VII, the Barotse had become well-versed in British Royalty. The official-looking medallion emblazed with the number "10" could certainly have been deceiving. Mamba could not read beyond the images, and the hustler had clearly known that, spinning a believable tale that these were newly issued ten-pound notes.

Tom was deflated and angry. He threw the roll of notes on the table in disgust.

"It is you who is the mampara. You have been tricked." sneered Tom as Mamba confusedly gathered the discarded notes in his trembling hands.

"You wrong, Bwana Tom. See ten-pound note," said the old man, his temper now rising, pointing emphatically to the gold medallion surrounding the number ten. Simalala rested a hand on his father's shoulder and shook his head. He had seen a British ten-pound note before and had learned to read a fair amount of English. As soon as Tom had stretched the label out on the table, Simalala knew that his father had been duped. He looked to Tom imploringly, who now paced with agitation.

"Alright. We can still get to them. They cannot move that fast with over two hundred heads of cattle. They will be using the path at the tsetse fly belt, it's the only belt wide enough to accommodate the passage of that many animals. That's if they're smart enough and want to keep them alive."

"I told them to use that path," said Mamba, now feeling the full sting of betrayal.

"Send your runners out ahead to track the cattle. We will follow behind and get them back," said Simalala confidently to his father. Mamba nodded in agreement, too ashamed to utter a word.

By sunset, they had only covered twenty miles. The initial excitement Maria had felt as they set off on the chase had now lost its thrill. She leaned her head on Tom's shoulder as they bumped along slowly through the bush.

"They hamba[19] tsetsha,[20] Bwana Tom," said Simalala running back to the truck, which had now stopped.

"Don't worry, Simalala. They might have gijima[21], but we will catch them. They don't know we are coming up behind them. But we

---

[19] Go
[20] Quickly
[21] Run

are all tired, so let's stop here and make camp tonight. They won't be moving either in the dark."

The Africans weren't in favor of traveling by night, so this arrangement suited everyone. They brought the truck to a halt in a clearing, and Tom, Simalala, and two Barotse men from the village, who had traveled with them in the truck, jumped out and began gathering supplies to make camp for the night. At his request, Maria had tucked herself under the blanket that Tom kept under the seat. The journey had been slow with Mamba and his entourage on foot.

But the old man's stamina was applaudable, and they trailed only a mile or so behind them. Simalala ran back to tell them that they'd stopped for the night, and they then followed suit, setting up their camp as well. By the time he returned, the crimson sunset had disappeared on the horizon, and the chilly night air was disturbed only by chirping crickets and the comforting crackle of a new fire.

"Thank you for my father. You are truly his friend. I pledge you my life, Bwana Tom. I promise you no harm will come to you, Miss Heidi, and your Dona." said Simalala earnestly across the fire from Tom as Maria emerged from the truck to join them.

Tom knew he meant it with every fiber of his being, and he was feeling guilty about insulting the old man.

"We will get them back, Simalala, don't worry. Now go be with him tonight," said Tom insisting Simalala spend the night at his father's camp. "And please encourage him to let me handle this when we find them." Simalala nodded, although both knew his father would want some sort of revenge.

After a simple dinner of biltong and some bread and jam that Maria had brought along in her trunk, they decided to turn in for the night. Not wanting to slow their progress the next morning, Tom had decided that they should sleep in the flatbed on the truck. He spread out two-bed rolls and gathered blankets from a crate he kept on board for such occasions. At the first roar of a lion in the distance, Maria abandoned her makeshift bed and crawled into the safety of Tom's arms. He didn't mind, as she nestled in close to him, sharing his small mattress. The night sky was blissful, she thought, deep and inky black dotted with little diamonds. But the sporadic rustling in the bush around them makes her edgy. Tom was tired, but he sensed her nervousness, so they lay awake for a while, whispering about what had transpired that day and what Tom's expectations were for the next until she finally fell asleep.

Tom woke Maria with a steaming cup of campfire coffee at daybreak.

"We need to get back on the trail Maria, so you might want to ready yourself." Tom looked anxiously at his wristwatch. It was six o clocks, and Simalala had already returned from Mamba's camp with news that they were ready to move. He was trying to be delicate, but time was against them. He knew that Maria probably needed to relieve herself and have some privacy to change. He had never traveled this far into the bush with a female, except Heidi when she was younger, and he was becoming acutely aware of how awkward this must be, being the only female in this whole troupe of men.

"If you want to get a change of clothes, I'll hold up a blanket over there by that tree, and you can…well, do what you need to do," Tom said awkwardly.

Maria smiled. She knew what he was getting at and took the offer gladly. He didn't know how self-sufficient she actually was and how it was only the bush that scared her, not the men. She rummaged through her trunk for a change of clothes and brought along a canister of talcum powder and a face cloth, stuffing everything into a small satchel.

"Can I get a little hot water from the kettle," she asked. "Of course," said Tom. "Follow me."

With her satchel and bowl in hand, they walked together to the edge of the clearing. Tom tied one corner of the blanket to a spindly branch of the huge baobab tree and stretched it eight feet across, holding the other end. Out of decency, he faced away from Maria towards the three African men gathered around the campfire, who was watching intently and stifling laughter at this ridiculous display of male subserviency.

Behind the blanket, Maria did her best with the warm wet face-cloth, powder, and fresh clothes and emerged no more than ten minutes later dressed in a light blue cotton sundress. Her hair had been combed, without the use of a mirror, and twirled into a tight bun at her neck. She still wore the same dirty boots from the day before, recognizing that they were just more practical given the circumstances. She tapped Tom lightly on the shoulder, and he dropped the blanket. He was duly impressed with her level of efficiency. With each minute, he was falling deeper, and it felt right.

They had been journeying now for over five hours, only taking one break mid-morning. The sun was blazing hot, even with the windows down, and Maria was grateful for her light clothing choice as she wiped the perspiration from her face with the cloth she had retained from that morning. The thieves were still illusive, and frustration was building in the ranks, as some of the men wondered if this expedition was futile. Mamba, however, remained completely focused, and so did Tom and Simalala, so they continued driving and walking in silence, consumed by their own thoughts.

Then in the distance, four African men came running at full speed towards them: Mamba's runners. Simalala jumped off the back of the truck and ran ahead to meet them. They had found them, about five miles up ahead came the message from the breathless four.

Invigorated by the news, the pursuers accelerated, and as expected, within half an hour, they could see the lingering dust cloud kicked up by the herd ahead. They waited for Mamba and his men to catch up. Upon seeing evidence of his cattle, Mamba took an assegai[22] in his right hand, and a great sjambok[23] in the other as his entourage of thirty men gathered around him, each with a spear at the ready. Tom, still seated behind the steering wheel, watched Simalala trying to argue with his father in the rearview mirror as the elder shouted orders to his men in Lozi.

"What are they talking about, Thomas?" asked Maria nervously.

---

22   Spear
23   Whip

"I have no bloody clue, but I'm about to find out," said Tom swinging open the door and heading towards the Barotse warriors.

"What's the problem now?" he said with a commanding voice. "You are my problem, Bwana Tom. I am going now with mypeople. You stay here with Simalala."

Turning to face his son, he sputtered in English. "You stay with the white man. You forget our ways. I will teach these white men a lesson. No one cheats, Mamba!" he emphasized his intentions with a crack of his sjambok.

Four men suddenly surrounded Tom and Simalala as Maria watched on from the truck window in horror. Out of desperation, she pulled Tom's revolver from the dashboard and pointed it out the window at Mamba.

"I will shoot you if you touch him, old man."

"It's alright, Maria. He won't hurt us. I promise. Just give him the gun." said Tom calmly, with exasperation.

Slowly Maria turned the gun over to one of Mamba's men, who was instructed to keep it safe. Tom could see that Mamba was fully consumed by fury, and he had seen what that fury was capable of.

"Now listen to me, Mamba. We will do as you ask and stay here. But you cannot kill them. They are white men, and they will be punished under white men's laws. Do you hear me? You cannot kill them, or you will pay the price."

Mamba's black eyes looked straight through him, and Tom wondered if any of what he was saying was registering. He was trying to protect the man from retaliation. But Mamba said nothing and left them standing there, guarded by his men.

"Bwana Tom, you don't worry. My father is angry because this is the second time he has been stolen from. He knows the laws of a white man, and he will not act stupid. Nothing will happen to the cattle thieves. He won't kill them." Simalala assured him, half believing his own words.

"I hope you're right, Simalala. And what about these men?" asked Tom glancing at the muscular deadpan warriors standing behind them.

"My father told them to hold us but not harm us."

"I'm sure Maria is scared. Can you tell them to let us all sit in the shade of that tree over there rather than standing here like fools?"

"They are simple people who are just as scared of you as you are of them, Dona," said Simalala trying to comfort Maria as the so-called guards acquiesced and escorted Maria out of the car to join them under the shade of the tree to wait.

Meanwhile, Mamba's men had caught up with the herd, which had stopped for water at the water pan. From the rear of the herd, Mamba took one of the fake notes from his belt and attached it to the assegai. Handing it to a young Barotse, he instructed him accordingly, and the youth hurled the spear with precision, injecting it into the earth next to the foot of a burly, blonde-bearded white man who stood at the front of the herd smoking a cigarette, completely unaware of the impending attack.

The bearded man shouted a warning to one of his partners bathing in the pan, who couldn't hear him from a distance. The herdsmen, a group of Tonga boys that were scattered amongst the cattle, fled the scene, scurrying in every direction, pursued by a handful of Barotse. By the time the bearded man had got his bearings, the Barotse had already rounded up the rest of his party, which included an older, heavy-set man with a large belly, the smaller dark curly haired man who had been swimming in the pan, and a younger man, who had been sitting alone in the shade of a tree a few yards ahead, next to their scotch cart full of supplies, and their bush truck.

The Tonga boys were gathered into a group under the guard of two imposing-looking Barotse men. The white men were all thrown into the dirt before Mamba. They were unarmed, all their rifles sitting unattended in their scotch cart. They didn't dare fight back; they were out-manned and out-weaponed. Six Barotse aligned themselves behind the thieves, prodding the blades of their assegais into the small of their backs. Mamba picked up the blond man's half-smoked cigarette and pressed it to his lips, inhaling it casually. After a few long puffs, he flicked the remains to the ground and crushed the burning stub with his bare foot, earning a gulp from the group's leader. With his assegai dug into the ground beside him, he ordered.

"Tonga will walk my animals back to the village."

Then retrieving the roll of useless condensed milk labels from his belt, he waved them angrily at the group of thieves at his feet and bellowed.

"You think you can cheat me? No! You don't cheat me. Tell me the name of who did this, and I will kill him instead of you."

The men exchanged glances with one another. One of the men, the squirrely curly-haired one, quickly relented, "It was Bradley. He gave us these to give you." Earning him a scowl from the bearded man.

"Who is this, Bradley? I know of no white man with the name Bradley."

The large man, in fear for his life, piped up, speaking in a thick Afrikaans accent. "He's a Brit…light hair…in his thirties. He had a mole on his cheek."

"What is a mole?" asked Mamba, searching his men for an explanation while they responded with shrugs.

"A mole… you know, like a dot, a black circle on the face. Right here." explained the fat man pointing to his right cheek.

The realization slowly set in. "I know this man. He is the man with the evil black dot on his face who stole my coins many years ago."

The Afrikaner chimed in again. "Call him what you want. Bradley or Black Dot, but I'm telling you, min, he is the one who gave us these notes. Just take your cattle and let us be."

"But he was your leader...this Bradley, this black dot man? If you do not speak my name to your policy, I will not kill you. But you tell him that I know who he is and what he has done." stated Mamba fueled with a vengeance at this revelation.

"Please just leave us be. We will deliver your message to Bradley." implored the bearded man on behalf of the company.

"But you must learn a lesson first," said Mamba with authority.

Mamba spoke no more to the white men but turned his back. In Lozi, he ordered them to be stripped, have their wrists tied above their heads, and be strung up on the nearest tree. When the men were hanging naked from the tree branch, Mamba's men were ordered to confiscate their belongings. All their clothes and supplies were taken down to the water pan and thrown into the water. Their rifles and anything deemed useful to Mamba were placed in the scotch cart, which began to make its trek back to the village.

Mamba's desire to salvage his reputation, especially with his men, was still unfulfilled. So, before he departed the scene, the old man circled behind each of the naked white men and whipped them with his sjambok once, then twice, then thrice to make sure their cries would carry, and they would never forget his name or the Barotse. The sjambok was punishing, and each body dripped blood from the lashes that spanned their backs from neck to buttocks. They moaned in collective agony. Mamba was satisfied.

In one final act of spontaneous retaliation, he had his men set their truck on fire, which boomed loudly as the fuel tank exploded, sending thick gray smoke into the air, scattering birds and small animals in every direction. Then Mamba gathered his men and, together with the young Tonga herdsmen, led his great herd back in the direction of the village, leaving the white men for Tom to manage.

The scotch cart, led by one of Mamba's men and filled with rifles, food, and other supplies, soon wandered into the clearing where Tom, Simalala, and Maria waited patiently. They had already heard the explosion and seen the gray smoke rising above the trees from a distance and were anxious for news.

"What trouble has the old bastard stirred up now? Does he want to start a wildfire?" said Tom jumping to his feet, followed by Maria and Simalala.

Tom's outburst earned him a gentle poke from an assegai, and they all sat back down. Within minutes a few cattle began to enter the clearing, and the guards relinquished their duties to herd the animals, deeming that more important. Mamba and the rest of the men soon followed. Mamba stood before Tom, who was back up on his feet again, and without a word, he placed his revolver in his hand and continued to his village with his men and herd in toe.

"Hey, where do you think you are going, you crazy old man?

What did you do out there?" Tom growled after him.

Turning, Mambo spoke calmly, "I do nothing but set their truck on fire and take their clothes. My sjambok cut their flesh, but I do not kill them. I know your law. But the police will not come to look for me. They will not speak my name. They will take my name to the man who cheated me."

"And my son…" Mamba said sternly to Simalala." "You let white man make you weak, but later you will understand why I teach them a lesson. I go now before my cattle get scared of fire."

"Hey, wait, did you find out who the man was…the one who tried to cheat you?" Tom called after him.

"Black dot man," answered Mambo. "The same one that cheated me the last time."

"Black dot man?" queried Tom, who had never actually met Bradley in person to get the correlation.

"Yes, they call him Bradley. He has an evil black dot on his face."

The sting of his response hit Tom in the gut. Everything now made sense. Bradley had planned to sabotage him all along, right under his nose. But that still didn't explain why he wanted Demberra.

"Bwana, we should go and check on the men," said Simalala urgently as soon as his father was out of earshot.

"Yes, yes, of course," said Tom, still gob-smacked.

Since the other men who had previously accompanied them had returned to the village, only Tom, Simalala, and Maria remained in the clearing. They all climbed back into the truck and pressed forward to find the victims of Mamba's wrath.

"Are you alright, Thomas," asked Maria

"I'm fine," said Tom lying.

"You look like you've seen a ghost." she pressed.

"It's just that I have a business arrangement with Bradley…it's complicated…I'll fill you in later."

The smell of burning diesel affronted their senses before anything else, as the carcass of a truck burned in the middle of the road up ahead. In the distance, they could see what looked like bodies hanging from a tree. Maria gasped.

"Now I warn you, Maria, this is not going to be pretty," said Tom bracing her for the worst.

They stopped the car and approached the tree. The four naked, bloodied bodies dangled a few feet from the ground lifelessly, like sacks of maize. Even in Mamba's old age, he had spared no mercy, and the gashes on their torsos were deep, as blood still trickled from the open wounds.

Simalala wasted no time cutting the ropes as the bodies collapsed to the ground beneath. Quickly, Tom wrapped the young man in a blanket as he murmured a delirious word of thanks. He was semi-conscious and probably, at this point, unable to feel the intensity of his pain. When Simalala tried to untie the ropes on the bearded man's hands, he lashed out, almost punching him in the face.

"It's alright, he's with me." qualified Tom as the man tried to stagger to his feet, still rife with rage.

"I thought we were going to bleddy die here, min." said the Afrikaner, helping his curly-haired friend to his feet, who offered groans of thanks.

Maria had already taken all the first aid supplies out of their vehicle and laid a couple of blankets under the tree, one for them to sit on and one for them to cover their nakedness. She had poured cups of water for all the men, which the men gulped enthusiastically once they were all gathered on the blanket, too much in pain to care about their lack of clothing. Maria treated their wounds with Dakin's solution, as the men winced and called out in pain as the liquid stung their open flesh. Once the wounds were clean and dressed, she bandaged them up as well as she could while Tom and Simalala retrieved their clothing from the banks of the water pan and put them out to dry on the hood of their truck.

Maria immediately took to the young man, who she estimated could be no more than seventeen or eighteen. He had a slim but athletic build, piercing green eyes, and thick dark wavy hair. He wasn't rough like the others and seemed out of place with this band of criminals. Maria had the distinct impression that he had been caught up in something beyond his expectations.

Tom had given the men each a few shots of whisky to dull their senses after the initial shock had worn off and the pain began to set in. The blonde, who they came to know as Hansie, and the Afrikaner, Juan, and his curly-haired Greek friend, Max, sat together under the tree, talking in muffled conversation. After their initial words of gratitude, Tom did not engage them further, and they made no effort to speak to Tom or Simalala either. They had saved them from certain and eventual death, thought Tom. He would make sure that they were returned to Livingstone alive. As far as he was concerned, that was all he owed them to keep the police out of this affair. Mamba had already bought their silence, or at least he hoped they would abide by their agreement. Soon enough, Bradley would know that his plan had been thwarted and that Tom knew all about it. It would change things.

Maria and the young man sat apart from the others in the truck with the windows down for the cross breeze. She liked how he referred to her as Mrs. Sutton. He was British, she had learned, and his father was a reputable government officer back in Salisbury. He said that he knew nothing about the cattle sham and had only taken up the adventure to explore the bush, being new to Africa. He seemed to be ashamed of his involvement in the matter, and she believed him. She asked about the scar on his leg, which still ran deep and red. When the young man affirmed that it was from a motorcycle accident, Maria reprimanded him like a mother would scold a son.

She somehow felt protective of him. Maybe it was his youth, or maybe she saw something in his naivete and vulnerability as a stranger in a strange land. He admitted to her that he had no real friends in Livingstone, where he was staying, and Maria promised she would write to him and that someday, perhaps, when this all blew over, he might come to visit them in Demberra.

As the afternoon trudged on and the men rested, Simalala showed Tom how to construct a grass bed that they could use as a canopy with poles. Once the men's clothes were dry, Maria and Tom helped them dress, thinking it best that Simalala keeps his distance for his own safety. They laid them all gently on a pile of blankets in the back of the truck. Simalala's grass canopy was hoisted above them to provide shade, and the poles were tied to the four corners of the flatbed. Simalala sat on the back of the truck, his legs dangling over the edge, out of the shade of the canopy, to keep watch over them. He had Tom's revolver by his side as a precaution.

"Where are you taking us?" growled Hansie

"To Kabi Siding. From there, you can get the train back to Livingstone," said Tom curtly as he and Maria gathered up their things and got back in the cab.

As the truck lurched forward, the men groaned in agony as the unforgiving road beneath them jostled them painfully from side to side. In the hours that ensued, all four of them scowled at Simalala, and at one point, the bearded man even constructed a plan to kick him from the vehicle, when Simalala said casually with a smile. "I can understand English, Bwana." Eventually, they concluded that it wouldn't be prudent to harm the man since he must be the servant of the white man who had rescued them, and right now, they couldn't jeopardize their rescue.

With each groan from the rear, Maria screwed up her face like she was vicariously feeling their pain, she could hardly bear it. Tom, on the other hand, was driven by a burning desire to get back to Demberra as fast as he could without inflicting any more unnecessary suffering on these men. He wished them no further injury, but he couldn't forgive them either for taking part in a ruse that was ultimately designed to destroy him. His grip clenched tighter on the steering wheel. This was going to be a long day.

CHAPTER 11

DECEPTION

Maria fell in love with Demberra at first sight. It was more magnificent than Tom had let on, not because the house was extravagant. It was a fair size, well decorated, and equipped with all the modern amenities she had become used to at Weasel's place. And Tom had also recently purchased a rotary phone and tapped into the phone lines, which was enviable in these parts. But it was not the house, the furniture, or creature comforts, and it was the pink bougainvillea that climbed the pagoda and surrounded the expansive verandah, Heidi's now robust vegetable garden, and the land itself that won Maria's heart.

The lushness of the rich, fertile ground reminded her of Mozambique, and she understood why this place meant so much to Tom. From ground to livestock, life was brimming all around them at Demberra. Even the little village that had cropped up on the ranch since Tom had taken over old Van Wyk's place seemed satiated and happy in this locale. Maria would never forget the happy faces of the farm workers' children, who greeted her that first day when they arrived.

It was also obvious to Maria, from the moment she had reached the top of the hill upon arrival, that this place had been touched by a woman, Tom's ward, Heidi. She had yet to meet the illusive girl, who she had come to know through stories and photographs. Heidi had been living in Salisbury for almost two years now. An opportunity to extend her studies as a student teacher had materialized at the end of her first term, and she had made the decision to stay. Knowing that her uncle had brought a strange woman to live at Demberra with him had been the deciding factor, although she didn't speak of it to Tom.

Tom had made the journey to Salisbury the Christmas prior to seeing Heidi. Heidi requested he comes alone so that they could discuss "personal matters." Maria read between the lines and graciously remained at Demberra. She was honestly relieved to stay behind. Admittedly she felt awkward about her relationship with Tom and how Heidi might perceive her. But other than optics and a desire for a more formal commitment, Maria had no regrets. Her love for Tom had not waned over the past two years, and she was sure that Tom loved her, too, in his way. She had even received Weasel's blessing after she had written him a long letter explaining why she had left and what Tom meant to her.

Here on the farm, she didn't have to put on appearances, and she liked that. The local Africans didn't seem to care that they weren't married. In fact, they often questioned why the Bwana didn't have two or three wives, as was their custom. However, she couldn't deny that it sometimes hurt not to be his wife. They were happy together and faithful to each other. She had hoped in time that Tom would ask her to marry him, and so she waited.

Over the past year and a half, Maria had made herself indispensable at Demberra. She had gladly taken over the running of the household, allowing Tom more time to tend to his growing farm. She spent countless hours in the kitchen, where she indulged Jonas in Portuguese recipes from her childhood and other exotic dishes, and quickly his reading and culinary skills blossomed under her tutelage. Soon he was mastering complicated recipes, utilizing all the fresh produce from their thriving garden.

Whether it was modern amenities, cars, or furniture, Tom and Maria both shared an excitement for new things, and food was no different. Even though it was just the two of them, dinners at Demberra would have been enviable by the most discerning epicurean.

Like Heidi, Maria also had a love for horses. After her mother died, Maria hadn't left her father's side, accompanying him on many a trade route. The most efficient mode of transport in those days was always horseback. So naturally, Maria fell in love with Soleil and cared for Heidi's horse as if it was her own while rekindling her joy of riding.

Tom and Maria frequently took trips to Livingstone, where she became acquainted with Len, Charlie, Bert, and even some of the local ladies. She was often invited to tea, while Tom spent the afternoon with Issy talking business or socializing on the verandah of the Northwestern with the men.

Tom had severed all communication with Bradley and his thieves, using Issy as a go-between if communication was required. After successfully purchasing Mamba's herd right after the theft attempt, he had worked tirelessly over the past year to meet his contractual agreement with Bradley, which would come due the following summer. Despite the occasional man-made bush fire and suspicious vagrant found milling around his property, none of which Tom could substantiate, Bradley had remained quiet.

For these reasons, Maria wasn't sure that Tom would have approved of her staying in touch with John, the young man they had rescued in the bush, despite the platonic nature of their relationship. It had started when Maria had penned a letter to his father to check in on his recovery following the cattle incident. His father had urged her to stay in touch, and so she had, exchanging letters every few months. John had even sent her a postcard from Spain the previous Christmas. The young man had wanderlust in his soul, and Maria knew that being detained at his father's house alone was probably taking a toll on his adventurous spirit.

In their letters, they spoke at length about their pasts. John seemed interested in her childhood, whereas Tom didn't care to talk too much about the past, especially Ireland or his childhood, except with Weasel. So, Maria didn't either in solidarity. But she enjoyed sharing the stories of her childhood in Portugal and her father's trade business with John in exchange for his tales of English Prep Schools and adolescent adventures in Paris with his chums. They also shared a common interest in modern music. John loved to talk about Swing music and filled Maria in on the latest great tunes that were on the radio in Europe and the States.

When she heard that the young man had recently returned to Livingstone, she was surprised. He had taken a job at the Livingstone bank and was letting a room in a house nearby. So, in the month or so leading up to Christmas, Tom and Maria made weekly trips to Livingstone. When Tom was busy attending to farm business, Maria would meet John for coffee at the little café near the bank where he worked instead of shopping or visiting with town friends.

There was nary a lull in their conversation. They picked up right where their letters had left off. She loved how he lit up when he rambled on about Glen Miller and Benny Goodman and how he dreamed of going to America someday. She loved his zest for life and desire to travel the world.

Maria also learned that he had lost his mother at a young age, although he shared a few details. This had affected him, and it was something he wouldn't talk about it. Maria intimately understood what that kind of loss could do to a young person, but it was obviously a compartment in his life that he wished to keep under lock and key. He was harboring some deep grief. Could it be trauma left over from the cattle incident? She wasn't sure, but she felt oddly responsible for him, although she wasn't more than eight years his senior. She only hoped over time that he might trust her enough to unburden himself.

As Christmas approached, Demberra lay in anticipation of Heidi's return. Tom, Maria, and Simalala had recently returned from Livingstone with a stockpile of supplies for the new year, gifts, and Christmas sweets for all the village children. The farm was bustling in preparation. Maria hoped and prayed that when they did meet, Heidi would see the care that she had taken to tend to her garden and her pony and ultimately recognize that she posed no threat to the bond Heidi shared with Tom.

That morning, she had decorated the house with bells and tinsel and had even set up a proper Christmas Tree on the verandah in honor of the season. Tom had set to work overseeing the upper fields, and when he bounded into the kitchen at noon, his shirt front was wet with sweat.

"Have you seen Simalala?" he asked Maria urgently as she stood chopping candied fruit to drop into the pot of simmering port for her Portuguese King Cake.

"He was up here at the house looking for you about half an hour ago. Why is there something wrong? You look worried." she said, putting down her knife and wiping her hands on her apron.

"There are cattle missing. Don't worry, and I'll sort it out," Tom replied with a quick peck on the cheek as he exited the side door.

"Hey, Simalala!" he shouted, seeing the man emerge from behind the stable. "Find the head cattle boy Simalala! He has some explaining to do. He is probably bloody drunk and hiding somewhere." Simalala nodded in agreement, leaned his rake against the wall, and disappeared to find the man.

Tom took a breather on the steps of the verandah, wiping his wet brow with the back of his sleeve.

"Here you are," said Maria offering him a cold glass of coke and joining him on the steps.

"Thanks, lass," said Tom, gratefully gulping down the fizzy drink.

"You're working very hard. Don't think I haven't noticed." Tom said coyly, brushing a strand of hair from her eye. "She's not going to bite you, you know." he laughed, but Maria only turned her gaze downwards.

"What is it? She knows all about you. And you are going to get along grand…wait and see."

"What does she think of us living here in sin, unmarried?" Maria asked tentatively, poking the taboo subject.

"Well, that's not her concern, is it?" Tom said grumpily as he rose and handed her his empty glass. "Thanks for the drink. I have things to attend to, and you best get back to your cake."

At that moment, Simalala reappeared, beckoning Tom to follow him. And just like that, the conversation was extinguished, and Maria was left to wonder what kind of future was in store for her here with Thomas Sutton, especially after his dear girl returned and assumed her rightful place as heiress and queen of this castle. She angrily pulled her hair back into a tight ponytail and returned to the kitchen to brood and bake.

The head cattle herder had been discovered in his hut, inebriated, reeking of African Chibuku beer. Simalala could not rouse the young man, who could barely stand. Tom frowned in disgust at the sight. The man lay on his sleeping mat, semi-conscious and soaking wet. His mouth was open, and saliva dripped down his chin. Despite being drenched in two buckets of water, the youth was barely conscious of their presence.

Tom reached down and yanked the man up by his dirty wet collar and bellowed in his face, "What the bloody hell happened to my sixty-eight cattle?

The man opened one eye and mumbled incoherently.

Simalala poured another bucket of water on the man, and he slowly staggered into a sitting position, cursing him under his breath.

"Bwana Tom. We did nothing. I even went and got the animal doctor when you were gone yesterday. The doctor says the Mombes were poisoned. We found many empty tins hidden by the dip tank. See right there, Bwana." The man said, trying to point in a semi-straight line to a pile of tins in the corner of his hut.

"The doctor said they were poisoned with ar-es-en-ic. When we saw the mombes stagger and fall after going through the dip tank, we stopped and tried to save the rest. It was bad water Bwana. We never do anything wrong, Bwana Tom."

Tom was furious, and he stormed out of the hut without a word to Simalala, he ran to the stable and saddled up his stallion quickly and took off westward at a gallop to the dipping tanks. Simalala meanwhile turned back his whimpering charge and gripped the man fiercely by his hair.

"You watch sixty-eight cattle die, and now you cry like a baby. I chop off your fingers, for you are not a man!"

The bite in his tone made the man flinch in fear. Simalala was a fair but intimidating Kapita, and he usually meant exactly what he Said. Simalala knew what this loss meant to Demberra' profitability and how this might ultimately put Tom's agreement with Bradley in jeopardy.

He sneered at the man once more, "Tell me what unknown Muntu came here when we were gone these three days?"

Silence.

Simalala tightened his fist around the man's hair and gave him one swift slap across the face. The man relented and divulged the names of four Africans in his drunken stupor.

Maria watched through the kitchen window as a small crowd of farm workers had begun to gather outside the house, as Simalala dragged the wet, drunk young laborer towards them. She came out on the verandah to join them and await Tom's return. Simalala filled her in on what had transpired. When Tom's horse Blackie came into view, the men moved to meet him. Tom dismounted, soaked through in sweat and blood red in the face with anger the likes they had never seen.

"What happened, Thomas? Is what the herder said true?"

Tom ignored her question and called the stable boy. "Rub him down well and make sure he rests a lot today." He said, handing over the glistening stallion.

"Thomas? What happened?" Maria asked again anxiously.

"He killed my cattle, that's what he bloody did, woman!" he growled, belittling Maria in front of all his workers. She paused for a moment like she was going to retaliate, but instead picked up the apron she had discarded on the chair without a word and rushed back into the house for fear that her tears would betray how wounded she felt. Tom did not follow her.

Tom knew he had hurt her, but he didn't have time for her feelings right now. Simalala briefed Tom on the names he had extricated from his drunk herder, and together they instructed the men to be on the lookout for any nefarious behavior. This was war. Simalala was in his element, and he had ensured Tom there would be retribution.

After the men had scattered, Tom slumped in one of the wicker armchairs on the verandah and helped himself to the bottle of scotch. He never drank during the day, but still, anger pulsed through his veins, and he wondered what he would do to Bradley if he stood before him right now. He was sure that this was his doing, but he had no way to prove it, at least not yet.

Maria didn't come out of the bedroom until dinner. The tension in the dining room that night was palpable. Neither of them spoke. Maria made sure to sit at the far end of the table opposite Tom to punctuate her displeasure.

Jonas' Duck, a l'orange, went completely unappreciated as the two lovers stabbed silently at the food with their forks. When dinner was over, Maria excused herself under the auspices that she had to monitor Jonas in the kitchen. When she could no longer avoid him, she found him on the verandah brooding and puffing a cigar. Tom knew that it was he that had to make amends.

When their coffee was served on the Mukwa table, they both came to sit down. Their hands touched as they reached for milk. She was beautiful even when she was angry, and he thought, smiling to himself. The night breeze fluttered against her black locks, which now hung loose down her back. Her bare feet were curled underneath her light cream silky caftan. She belonged here and deserved much more than he could give her, and he knew that. No longer able to stand the torturous silence between them, he cleared his throat.

"He's a good stallion."

Maria furrowed her eyebrows.

"Blackie. I am sorry for riding him beyond his capacity today."

Maria offered a small nod. This was not the explanation she was waiting for.

"Maria. Whatever happened this afternoon… I want to apologize for my…."

Maria interrupted, "you don't have to apologize to me, Thomas, I am not your wife."

Her words were like a gut punch.

"Maria, please don't say that. I love you. You know that. Is that not enough? And I am sorry…I would never want to hurt you."

Tom didn't wait for a response. The tears welling in her eyes were enough. In one swift movement, he lifted her from her seat as she fastened her bare legs around his waist. With lips pressed together, he carried her to their bedroom and closed the door gently. Apologies were made deep into the night with kisses and caresses, and for a time, Tom forgot the grave trouble they were in.

Tom awoke to Jonas' knock at the door at six am sharp. He was still stifling a yawn as he bid Jonas enter with his breakfast tray of buttered toast, homemade jam, and hot coffee. He had slept deeply last night, and Maria was only just beginning to rustle. They had both needed that night of reckless abandon to rid themselves of the tortures of the day. After Jonas had deposited the breakfast tray on the sideboard and exited, Tom propped himself up on his elbow to sip his coffee. His eyes surveyed Maria's peaceful sleeping frame as she turned away from him and fell back asleep. He put down his coffee and tried to inch himself closer to her, causing the cotton sheet to slip down to her waist, exposing her naked back. He needed her in his life. He needed her love and her comfort. He wanted her to stay with him. He placed a gentle kiss on the nape of her neck and whispered.

"Oh, my Maria, you are so beautiful. I am glad you are here with me. I will never want anyone else."

Tom quietly crept out of bed and made his way to the bathroom, his coffee in one hand and a slice of toast in the other. As soon as the bathroom door clicked shut, Maria rolled onto her back and stared at the ceiling.

"I love you too, my Thomas. So, make me your wife."

Out along the foot of the hill, a small but vigorous fire burned by the Kraal to combat the biting chill of the morning. Demberra's workers had gathered around it, warming themselves. It was a morning ritual that they all enjoyed, and Tom included, regardless of the season. On a typical day, the Bwana would arrive and lay out the plans for the day, discuss the farm and village's supply needs and hear any grievances or complications from Simalala on behalf of the men. But today was not a typical day. They were effectively all Mamparas[24] today, or at least that is what Simalala had called them. The farm had suffered an enormous loss, and they all expected to be interrogated about the poisoning. Each man would be questioned by Tom or Simalala before they would be allowed to share their sentiments or opinions on the matter. They all agreed that this witan-like assembly provided a sense of justice. It was a place where they all could be heard on even the most menial subject, and it had become a staple at Demberra.

Tom waited for Simalala's arrival, but when the man failed to come, he began the assembly but launching into his usual lecture these days about the importance of heightened vigilance and expedient communication during these uncertain times. Somewhere in his speech, he noticed that the men were not looking at him but focusing their attention on the distance behind him.

Cupping his forehead to shelter it from the morning sun, Tom turned and saw the figure of a tall, lean African man about two hundred yards in the distance being escorted towards them by Simalala. Every time the man tripped and fell to the ground, Simalala would promptly kick him in the backside. When they reached Tom and the assembly, Simalala proudly kicked the man like a dog until he landed at Tom's feet. He looked up at Tom in defiance with one blue eye, and the other was covered with a patch of cloth.

"What's all this about," asked Tom deliberately.

"Tell Bwana the truth!" snarled Simalala jerking the man up by the collar of his shirt.

No answer came.

"Will you just tell me what's going on?" Tom bellowed. Simalala gritted his teeth at the man and spat in anger.

"I spent all night looking for him, Bwana, and I find him down the rail. I make sure he talks to you."

---

[24] Fools

Simalala grabbed the man again, pulling him to his feet. His one blue eye surveyed the crowd. He was outnumbered, and his eye darted left to the right, waging his chances or lack thereof.

Accepting his lack of options, the man broke his silence. He verified what Tom had already assumed. Bradley, the white man with the mole, had hatched the entire scheme. By poisoning his cattle, he intended to cripple Tom financially. Once the rainy season was upon them, Tom wouldn't be able to make the trek to buy more cattle, even if Mamba had more to sell. If he couldn't honor the timeframe of the contract, Bradley would undoubtedly become the new owner of Demberra, and he and Heidi would lose everything. He had callously used Africans to do his dirty work and had paid them handsomely, so he could keep his hands clean legally. The court would never believe a black African man over the word of a white man.

Tom's blood pulsed faster through his veins, and his heart threatened to beat right out of his chest. His worst fear had been confirmed, and he now understood that Bradley would stop at nothing until he got what he wanted. But he still couldn't fathom why the man wanted Demberra so much that he would go to these lengths to sabotage him. It just made no sense.

He instructed Simalala not to mistreat the blue-eyed man. He was to be kept in their custody as a vital witness, whatever that might mean in a court of law. He instructed all the men to be on the lookout for any foul play and to report any suspicious activity directly to Simalala. He took six of his most trusted workers and put them in charge of patrolling different parts of Demberra, from the house to the village and fields, crops, and corrals. He was off to Livingstone that night to put an end to this.

Tom would not wait for the train this time. He had his car pulled around and gave Maria explicit instructions to phone him at Northwestern if Simalala reported anything out of the ordinary.

"You know where the shotgun is, right?" he asked her seriously.

"Yes, Thomas."

"Good girl. I know you know how to use it. You'll be fine, and I've asked Simalala to check in on you."

"How long will you be," Maria asked

"No more than two days. I'm ending this thing with Bradley once and for all."

"Thomas, please be careful."

"I promise," said Tom sincerely and kissed her goodbye, climbing into his Lancia Lambda Torpedo.

Tom pulled into Livingstone still in a fury, three and half hours later, road dust in his hair and sweat on his brow having done record time. He first stopped at Issy's. In breathless bursts, he told him the whole story as Issy listened intently. He was short one hundred and fifty pounds, but fearing what Bradley was capable of, Issy didn't hesitate. Out of his safe, he handed Tom the money.

"End this, Tom! For all your sakes."

"I will pay this all back to you, Issy, by the summer," said Tom earnestly, tucking the cash in an envelope with his other money.

"I know you will. Here, take the contract and make sure he signs it and make sure you keep a copy."

"Thank you, Issy. I owe you one," said Tom taking the contract and swiftly exiting his office.

"Don't hurt him, Thomas," called Issy after him, but he was gone.

He pulled his car up right outside Bradley's office. He had never met the man before since he had had everything explicitly handled through Issy's office. He took a deep breath outside his office door. He had to keep his temper in check, as much as he'd like to lay waste to the scum. He did not bother to knock but stormed right in, causing Bradley to reel around in his seat in surprise. Max, the curly-haired man from the cattle incident, was the first to react, rising defensively from his seat. He became the first target of Tom's wrath. Tom pulled Max from his seat by his belt and disposed of him down the office entry stairs like a child's plaything.

"Don't get involved. Or by God, you'll end up with broken bones too!" said Tom to Max as he began to peel himself off the floor.

"Are you mad, Sutton?" Bradley sneered with a condescending tone as Max got to his feet and brushed off his trousers, then climbed the stairs, careful to keep at least a six-foot distance from this mad Irishman.

"Oh no, Bradley, you little shit, I am of firm mind and body. I'm just a little upset that you had my cattle poisoned, is all." said Tom dripping with sarcastic venom. Bradley's eyes widened at the revelation, and he could not hide his fear.

"Yes, one of your bought Muntu ratted you out after my Kapita got a hold of him. I believe you owe me sixty-eight cattle, Bradley." insisted Tom sealing his request with a punch to the gut. Bradley hit the floor and gasped for air.

"I suppose you don't like fighting men, eh Bradley. You only like preying on women." scoffed Tom in reference to the numerous stories he'd heard of Bradley's reputation and the rumors Bradley had spread about him. Bradley only moaned in response.

Satisfied with Bradley's condition, Tom picked him up by the collar of his starched pinstripe suit and dumped him back into his brown leather swivel chair. Tom gestured to Max to take the other seat, and he did timidly. The assaulted man tamed his breath and ran his hand through his perfectly coiffed blond hair. Looking at him across the desk, his mole was quite evident, and now he understood how the Africans might have seen that as an evil omen. He did indeed live up to the namesake.

"Alright, alright. I will give you fifty pounds for the cattle." he finally admitted breathlessly.

"Come to think of it. You will pay exactly what I ask; one hundred pounds," said Tom with a threatening grin.

"Don't push your luck, Sutton."

"Oh, believe me, I'm not pushing mine. But you lad is in no condition to negotiate. Remember that old man you stole from, called Mamba? He knows well who and where you are. He's just biding his time, that's what the Lozi do you see. And believe me, and he will do unthinkable damage to you, more than my poor Irish sensibilities could even conjure. So, you're not just going to pay me for the cattle, and you are going to pay him back the exact number of gold sovereigns you stole and compensate him for the cattle you attempted to steal from him.

Look, I'm doing you a favor. I could have just left your men, like Max, here to Mamba's wrath. But see, I don't want the old man going to prison for killing the likes of you and your ilk. I have enough shit on you now to go to Len Johnston, so you are going to meet my demands."

"So, what is, Sutton?" asked Bradley with agitation.

"Here is what I owe you, a full seven months early. You are going to release Demberra and sign over the deed for the King's property. Here is the contract stipulating that you have been paid in full and no longer retain the rights to either property. Sign it!"

Bradley stared at him.

"Go ahead and count it. I'll wait," said Tom taking the other office chair. He sat and casually put his feet up on Bradley's desk, being careful to knock the dirt from his boots all over it in the process.

Bradley was in survival mode and was aware of the leverage Tom had on him. He had been outmaneuvered, at least for now. He had no choice but to accept the cash and sign the contract.

With his copy in hand, Tom rose, put on his hat, and made his way to the door.

"Oh, one more thing, Bradley. I'll take the cash now for the sixty-eight prime bullocks of mine that you poisoned."

Bradley scowled again but had no choice in the matter. He rifled through the cash Tom had just given him and handed him back one hundred pounds. Tom smiled with satisfaction and stored the cash in his inside jacket pocket.

"Just a second there, Sutton," Bradley demanded as Tom pushed the door of his office to leave.

"As sad as it may be to you kaffir loving Irishman, you must know that it will be my word against that crazy old kaffir's. And you don't really suppose that the nice white magistrate, at whose home I dine every Sunday, would believe him over a fine British gentleman like myself, now do you? My three men will gladly take the blame, for the right price, of course, and deny I was ever involved. As for the poisoning, your evidence is thin and again based on the word of kaffir. I just don't want the aggravation."

"Don't mess with me, Bradley. You can go ahead and make your predictions and assumptions, but we are finished here. Just do as I say and pay the old man what you owe him. If you settle your debt, maybe you'll remain in one piece."

Bradley flattened the creases in his shirt and sat back down in his chair, and reached for a cigarette. Tom watched as he slowly lit it and inhaled.

"I won't be trying anything with you personally, Sutton," said Bradley through an exhalation of cigarette smoke. "See, I value my reputation. You are simply a thorn in my path. And all thorns can be plucked and removed in good time."

Tom didn't know what to make of his cryptic prediction. He had got what he had come for, and as far as he was concerned, this deal was over. He hoped he would never lay eyes on the man again.

"Say hello to your woman, Maria, is it? And your beautiful young ward Heidi for me," added Bradley as he licked his upper lip. He knew that Tom had what he wanted and wouldn't jeopardize his prize with any retaliation now.

"Step one foot on Demberra, and you'll regret it. Mark my words." sneered Tom as he slammed the office door, nearly breaking the glass in the pane.

Tom tried to put Bradley's threat from his mind and headed to Northwestern for a shot of whiskey to calm his nerves. Early the next morning, he went straight to Issy and paid him half of what he owed him, keeping the remainder for operating costs and supplies for the coming month. Paying the rest of Issy's loan wouldn't be a challenge, and his friend was chumped to have so much of the loan paid back so quickly. After the contract and deed were officially registered at the courthouse, Tom left Livingstone.

With the windows open and his foot on the gas pedal, he sped home, sucking in the hot African air and filling his lungs with hope. He had done it! In his pocket, he held not only the deed for Demberra but also for the King's property. For the first time since his involvement in the Irish underground movement, he felt proud of himself and worthy of this success.

Heidi would be home within the week, and he couldn't wait to tell her that he had preserved her position as the rightful heir of Demberra and more. Her future was secure. Despite their apprehensions, he couldn't wait for the two most beloved women in his life to meet. This Christmas would be one he would never forget.

To be continued…